A Lover's Discourse

Village of Stone
A Concise Chinese–English Dictionary for Lovers
20 Fragments of a Ravenous Youth
UFO in Her Eyes
Lovers in the Age of Indifference
I Am China
Once Upon a Time in the East
Nine Continents

Xiaolu Guo

A Lover's Discourse

Grove Press
New York

Jacket design and illustration © Suzanne Dean incorporates Woman, Bonfanti Diego © Getty images; Man, DEEPOL by Plainpicture/Oleksii Karanov; illustrations of black elderberry by Mary Eaton © National Geographic/Bridgeman; Swallow © Bridgeman; Wasp by John Curtis © Bridgeman Images and Elderberry by Walther Muller from Hermann Adolph Koehler's Medicinal Plants © Florilegius/Bridgeman

From *A Lover's Discourse* by Roland Barthes. Published by Jonathan Cape Reprinted by permission of The Random House Group Limited © Roland Barthes 1979. From *Empire of Signs* by Roland Barthes. Copyright © Skira., 1970. Translation Copyright © Farrar Strauss and Giroux. First published in Great Britain in 1983 by Jonathan Cape. Reprined by permission of The Random House Group Limited.

'Raindrops Keep Fallin' On My Head' Words and Music by Hal David and Burt Bachrach © 1969 BMG Gold Songs (ASCAP) / New Hidden Valley Music Co. (ASCAP) All Rights Administered by BMG Rights Management (US) LLC. Used by Permission of Hal Leonard Europe Limited. All Rights Reserved. © 1969 WC Music Corp. (ASCAP) Licensed courtesy of Warner Chappell Music Ltd.

'Wind of Change' Words & Music by Klaus Meine© Copyright 1997 BMG Rights Management GmbH BMG Rights Management (UK) Limited, a BMG Company.

All Rights Reserved. International Copyright Secured.
Used by permission of Hal Leonard Europe Limited.

Published simultaneously in Canada
Printed in the United States of America

First Grove Atlantic Hardcover edition edition: October 2020

Library of Congress Cataloging-in-Publication data is available for this title.

ISBN 978-0-8021-4952-7
eISBN 978-0-8021-4954-1

Grove Press
an imprint of Grove Atlantic
154 West 14th Street
New York, NY 10011

Distributed by Publishers Group West

groveatlantic.com

20 21 22 23 24   10 9 8 7 6 5 4 3 2 1

Language is a skin: I rub my language against the other. It is as if I had words instead of fingers, or fingers at the tip of my words. My language trembles with desire.

—*Fragments d'un discours amoureux,*
Roland Barthes

A Lover's Discourse

Contents

Prologue

Love at first sight is a hypnosis.
—Roland Barthes

– I don't believe in love at first sight.
– What do you mean? Wasn't it clear the moment you
picked the elderflowers by the park and we looked at each
other? Or was it in that book club?

A few years after we moved in together, we had this conversation about love at first sight. I remember you said:

'I don't believe in love at first sight.'

I was taken aback. I thought we were definitely in love at first sight.

'What do you mean? Wasn't it clear the moment you picked the elderflowers by the park and we looked at each other? Or was it in that book club?'

You gave me a damp smile, as if my confusion proved that you were right.

But doesn't love always start from first sight? I mean, before one reaches one's thirties or forties. It's only when we have a second thought about our first sighted love, that we might change our mind. You might ask, why does this happen before one reaches midlife? I don't have a theory yet, but I think when we are young, our impulses take over our mind. Romantic love is always an impulse in my case.

I am not old or wise enough to understand yet what else love could be.

All I knew in that first moment at the park was that you saw the way I had looked at you. Perhaps I should not be so sure that you saw how I looked at you. Well, you were still a complete stranger. You were from a culture I had no knowledge or deep understanding of. Besides, you were very tall and I was short. Height sometimes disorients our perspective.

ONE

西

WEST

The Elderflowers

– What will you do with them?
– The elders? I will head them and boil them up.

I didn't know your name when we first met. No one introduced us. The only thing I remember is that you were picking roadside elderflowers.

We were in a park, Clapton Pond in north-east London. Some friends had arranged a picnic to celebrate a warm spring. But on that day, it was neither sunny nor warm. The clouds above London were making fun of us, with their fluffy cotton faces. The daffodils had faded, but the bluebells had just begun to bloom. Their clustered buds were nodding in the wind. Everyone was talking. And I was watching. Words didn't come so naturally to my mouth. The English manner was something I found difficult to follow then. You were the only man who was not involved in any of the conversations. You walked away from us, and disappeared behind some shrubs by the roadside. I could see you were plucking milky-coloured plants by the edge of the park. When you came back, I saw that you were carrying a bunch of elderflowers. You glanced at me, with a look I could not quite read. Your eyes were blue green, and they didn't dart about but were steady. I was not used to seeing a man holding wild flowers on an occasion like this. I thought there was perhaps something socially peculiar about you, or at least a little eccentric. Still, you had an air of normality. I noticed your blue denim jacket, and your muddy boots.

'What will you do with them?' I asked, pointing at the flowers.

'The elders?' you answered. 'I will head them and boil them up.'

You remained in my memory as *the elderflower picker*. Even though I later learned that men (especially European men) do pick wild flowers sometimes. But that day in the park was only a few months after I came to Britain, and I had never seen a man do that with such concentration in public.

You were the elderflower picker. And that is how I still picture you, after all these years.

Vote Leave

– It says Vote Leave, *but leave what?*
– Oh, leave the EU! You know, the European Union.

I came to Britain in December 2015, six months before the Referendum. I had no idea there would be a referendum. I vaguely knew this word in a Chinese context. But in China we never had such an experience. I had never voted, because we were never asked to vote. Besides, we were told only countries like Switzerland or Iceland might be able to conduct a national referendum because of their tiny populations. Leaving aside politics, I had too many unanswered questions for myself when I came to England. After my MA in sociology and film-making in Beijing, I didn't want to work in an office, nor did I want to stick around in China. I read a biography of the American anthropologist Margaret Mead, and decided to study visual anthropology in the West. I wanted to be a woman in the world, or really, a woman of the world – I wanted to equip myself with an intellectual mind so that I could enter a foreign land and not be lost in it. I would have a stance or mission, a way of navigating as an outsider. So I applied for PhD scholarships, and finally King's College London accepted me.

So here I was. I had arrived in the deep winter. It was cold, and mostly grey.

I had booked a small Airbnb in south London for the first few weeks, and thought I would be able to walk to King's College since it was close to the South Bank. I laughed myself to tears when I found out the distance was so great. It was almost impossible to walk in this city. There were hardly any straight avenues or boulevards one could orient oneself with, and the pavements were an uncomfortable public space to walk on. Once I almost tripped over what I took to be a pile of laundry, before I saw it was an occupied sleeping bag, a homeless person. Making my way through the dense city was like walking a tightrope strung across a raging torrent of traffic. It was so overwhelming that I chose to use the bus instead and perch myself by the window to view the world.

Two and a half months had passed, and I moved to accommodation in east London. One morning, I was on a bus on my way to see my supervisor. I saw a poster with the word *Brexit*. I didn't know what it meant. I hadn't read any English newspapers since I arrived. I checked the word in my pocket Chinese–English dictionary. Oddly, it was not there. The traffic was bad. We were stuck in streets which were lined with other buses. Right beside us, a red bus stopped. There were no passengers on it. A slogan on the side read:

We send the EU £350 million a week
let's fund our NHS instead
Vote Leave

I studied it for a while, and with my adopted anthropological spirit I wrote it down and photographed it. I pondered on the slogan. I had heard of the NHS – something to do with everyone getting free medical care in Britain.

While I was scratching my head, I heard someone behind me say:

'Look, there's one of those stupid Brexit Buses again!'

'Oh no!' his friend responded, turning to look. 'Will anyone believe this bullshit?'

I thought this could be my opportunity to interview a few natives. So I stoked up my courage, and asked in my most polite way:

'Excuse me, what is a Brexit Bus?'

'Sorry?'

The native informant stared at me, blankly. His friend laughed. I tried to hide my embarrassment. Clearly my question was stupid in some way. Nevertheless, I kept trying.

'Sorry, I just arrived recently. I'm new here.'

The native didn't bother to answer. He just shrugged dismissively.

But I was calm and cool, and didn't give up. 'It says *Vote Leave*, but leave what?'

'Oh, leave the EU! You know, the European Union,' he finally answered.

Oh, the European Union. For us Chinese, the European Union seemed grand. And in fact, deep down, we always wanted to be part of something like that. But apparently, some people here didn't want to be in it. Before I could continue my interview, we heard an announcement: 'This bus is on diversion. The next stop will be London Wall.'

I thought, London Wall? I knew of the Berlin Wall, but I had never heard of a London Wall. Was it also a Communist wall but between East and West London? With some curiosity, I got off the bus, and stood in a place called London Wall, but only found myself under a bleak-looking bridge with traffic lights in all directions. The Brexit Bus by then was gone too. Now I had to walk, but in which way?

Family History

– What's your family history?
– Why do you want to know?

In the beginning I was very lonely.

I thought it was obvious I would be lonely. I had just come to Europe. But I asked myself: had I always felt lonely even when I was in China? Even when my parents were around? Yes, I had. Maybe because I was an only child. Or maybe because the burden of study had killed any other kind of life. But here it was different. Here it was the feeling of desolation. Evenings were difficult to pass. English nights were long, and they didn't belong to the non-pub-going people. Nor did they belong to foreigners, especially those friendless and familyless foreigners. What were we supposed to do at night in our rented rooms, if we didn't drink or watch sports?

There was an area by the canal I often passed on foot. It was a little green patch next to De Beauvoir Town, by a lock-keeper's cottage. I didn't know how many lock-keepers' cottages were in use by Regent's Canal. And I never managed to walk all the way along the canal. I was afraid to walk through the grim part of it. I didn't trust it. But around this cottage I had a certain feeling of homecoming. So I went back there one evening, with my bag full of library books and a packet of biscuits.

The cottage was minute, as if it were built for dwarfs. There was neither a lock-keeper nor anyone else living in it. It was always locked. There were some dead sunflowers by the wall. I sat on a tree stump next to a wild nasturtium bush, and my eyes fixed on the rusty water. It was not that I could see the nasturtiums but I could smell them. We used to eat their peppery leaves as well as their sour-tasting flowers in my home town. My mother would pick them. So with that peppery smell in the air I knew what plant I was sitting next to.

A small waterfall was rushing down from the upper level of the canal. The sound was loud, but peaceful. In the near distance, the lights were on in one of the boats. A warm glow in the grey green. It was a mournful place. I never thought it was beautiful. For me, the idea of a beautiful scene was associated with a typical Chinese landscape – bamboo and water lilies by a temple, or a wild mountain. Never this kind of industrial landscape. But this lock-keeper's cottage and quietly flowing water soothed me somehow, made me feel less alien in this city.

As I was sitting there, staring at the water, my mind began to wonder. Should I just give up and fly back on the next plane? My parents were recently dead, so they could no longer say anything about it. Maybe my aunt would be surprised to see me return. But she had no say in my future life. You feeling lonely? It's too hard? Too cold? Were these real problems? Everyone in China would ask. For them, these were perhaps happy problems, since everyone in China was either dying of cancer or suffering from some traumatic family history. And their children would bear the weight of that wherever they went, even abroad.

I thought of the week before when I had first met my GP. I registered myself at the clinic and the GP asked me:

'What's your family history?'

I didn't understand why she had asked this. Because in China, the question of *family history* means whether you were born in a family whose status was either *peasant* or *city dweller*, and whether they were Communist Party members or not. These details were recorded officially throughout your life. And I didn't expect I would have to carry all this old baggage to England.

'Why do you want to know?' I didn't hide my irritation.

The GP was taken aback. She glared at me, then after a few awkward moments, she explained:

'Your family history is about whether your mother or your father had cancer, heart disease or rheumatism, or . . .'

I then understood what she was asking. I just nodded my head.

But the doctor was confused. 'So . . . what conditions, then?'

'Everything.' I nodded again. 'Everything you just said.'

'Everything?' she asked back, like I was a person with a low IQ.

'Yes, everything!' I raised my voice: 'Cancer, heart disease and rheumatism!'

A Desirable Immigrant

– *You are now a* desirable immigrant, *as they say!*
– *Ha, a* desirable immigrant! *Since when did I become an* immigrant?

The second time we met was a few days after that strange event – the Referendum. Clearly things were happening in this country, but I did not understand what they were. I remember walking around my neighbourhood the next day and seeing the looks on people's faces. Some looked tired and despondent and others a bit wild. This all added to my feelings of disorientation and confusion.

One day, an Englishwoman who worked in the university library mentioned in passing that I could join her for a weekend gathering. The pub was near where I lived. I said I would definitely come.

'What's the exact address in Hackney Down?' I asked her.

'Hackney *Downs*,' she corrected me.

At that time I didn't know *Downs* was a proper word, a meaningful word.

'It's a pub called People's Tavern – we'll meet there at five.'

When I got there that day, I saw the sign *Hackney Downs* by the park. I wondered about that word. Downs, not Down. Plural. Then I found you in the pub. I was surprised. Your curly hair, straw-coloured, was a little shorter than the first time I met you. Your eyes, the same blue green I remembered.

You recognised me too. I thought you were directing a slight smile towards me, but I could have been imagining it.

It was a book-club meeting. They say book clubs are for lonely people, or middle-aged women. I was definitely lonely, but neither of us was middle-aged. You were the only man in the group. Most women there were new mothers of small children. I didn't feel I could blend in. I didn't like the idea of having children, or marriage.

One of them was very pregnant and stated: 'I will probably never have time to read a book in the next few years.' She hugged her swollen belly.

Everyone had a copy of Doris Lessing's *The Golden Notebook*. But no one was eager to discuss it. Everyone was talking about Brexit. And I was beginning to understand what the word meant. Or at least some of the politics behind it. But the emotion remained alien to me.

A ginger-haired woman spoke: 'My daughter will grow up in a Brexit world, a non-European world as a European child. Can you believe it?' She looked distressed.

Another responded: 'Well, you have an Italian passport and an apartment in Rome, and they won't take these things away. You are now a *desirable immigrant*, as they say!'

'Ha, a *desirable immigrant*! Since when did I become an *immigrant*?'

'We are all foreigners here. No one is aboriginal!' The pregnant woman made another statement.

A desirable immigrant. I repeated this to myself. If I stayed, would I be one of the desirable immigrants? I wondered.

You didn't say much. The conversation was infused with a certain anger and intensity. It was interesting to watch, but difficult to follow. Then the group began to talk about housing and the property market. *The Golden Notebook* was left on the floor. Literature gave way to real estate. Everyone had so much to say about property, except for you and me. Were we connected by our mutual disconnection from these women?

Engländerin

– So where are you from? I can't tell if you have an accent.

– I grew up in Australia. Aber meine Mutter ist eine Engländerin, *originally.*

Then I called you. Because you hadn't called me. Not even once.

'I'm away this weekend, in Hanover,' you explained on the phone. 'But we can meet next week.'

Hang Over? I was puzzled. Was it a place? A hotel, or a famous bar?

But I dared not expose my ignorance. Instead, I asked: 'When are you coming back from Hang Over?'

'Oh, look, I don't drink that much. But I'll be back on Tuesday.'

Although your voice had a laughing quality, it had a calm and sober centre. I imagined you speaking on the phone from somewhere else in the city. But I could not picture what that place might look like.

'We can meet on Wednesday then. There is a Chinese restaurant in Old Street. How about we meet there for lunch?'

'Wednesday is a bit tight for me. But I can try,' you said. 'Hope the food isn't too spicy.'

I paused for a second, and thought you must be one of those hypersensitive northern Europeans who couldn't eat anything hot. You might even be a vegan, who eats tasteless food. No salt in your meals either, because of high blood pressure. I would find out.

So we arranged a time to meet. You suggested a very particular time – 12.45 – and you had to leave at 13.50 or just before 14.00. This sounded awful to me. Too precise. It was like going to see a dentist. It is true that you Westerners are not able to be spontaneous in your day-to-day lives, and you are from a supposed *free country*.

Wednesday arrived. You came into the restaurant wearing a battered leather jacket. Obviously you had not shaved. When we sat down at the table, you didn't appear to like what was on the menu: spicy cow's stomach, pickled duck tongue, ants on noodle trees, and so on.

'My grandmother used to make stews from pig guts and liver.' You stared at a colourful picture of fried stomach, slightly amused. 'I used to stuff myself with it when I was a kid. It was so chewy and tasty and I thought it was just meat. Then one day, when I was about nine or ten, I found out what those long tubes were. I never went near it again!'

'I know. Westerners think Chinese are inhuman. We kill anything just for eating. And we stir-fry anything alive.'

You didn't comment on this. Perhaps out of politeness?

'So, are you a vegetarian?'

You nodded. 'More or less.'

I began to worry. Perhaps there was nothing for you to eat in this restaurant. Plain rice with soy sauce? Were you also a gluten-free person?

A Chinese waitress stood by our table. She had the face of a terracotta soldier. Speaking Mandarin, I ordered some vegetables. She responded in Cantonese. You made a few interjections in English. When she left, I continued:

'Are you English?' For me, this fact needed to be confirmed, so I knew to whom I was talking.

'No way – I'm no Pom.' You laughed. 'That's what we used to say in Australia.'

I was puzzled. My monocultured Chinese education was manifesting itself again. 'What does that mean?'

'Look, basically I'm an Anglo-Saxon, a Wasp.'

'Wasp?' Now it was my turn to laugh. 'A fly with yellow-and-black stripes, going around stinging people?'

'I don't sting people, but I do wear striped shirts.' You choked a little on your hot green tea, then explained: 'A Wasp is a white Anglo-Saxon Protestant. You might have heard of it?'

'Hmm, a white Anglo-Saxon Protestant.' All these words sounded alien to me, apart from *white*. 'You know, every day I hear some new English words. I hear them but I don't register them. As if I was half deaf.'

You raised your eyebrows slightly. 'I know what you mean. I'm not from Britain either.'

'So where are you from? I can't tell if you have an accent.'

'I grew up in Australia, on the east coast. When I was eighteen, we moved to Germany. To cut a long story short, one morning my father woke up and announced that he wanted to go back to Germany.' Then you put on a German accent: 'I can do a German accent if I want to. *Aber meine Mutter ist eine Engländerin*, originally. That's me summed up.'

Mutter. Mother, I guessed. The rest remained opaque. I could see that Australia, Germany and England all had something to do with what you were. There was something mysteriously attractive about it.

And then this strange place you visited called *Hang Over*. It wasn't until a year later that I understood which city you meant. In China, we call it *Hannuowei*, a wealthy German city that produced the Scorpions, a band I had listened to when I was at university.

Morning Dew

– How swiftly it dries, the dew on the garlic-leaf.
The dew that dries so fast.
Tomorrow it will come again.
But he whom we carry to the grave will never return.

Near Haggerston station by the canal, there were two housing estates: De Beauvoir Town and Orwell Estate. They were massive, connected with long corridors and narrow green spaces, and shared the same architectural style. As I sat by the water, De Beauvoir Town was quiet right behind me. Even with multitudes of families living in these council homes, the estate felt strangely serene in the early morning. As did the canal before me. No wind. No human noise. Maybe because it was Sunday. It had rained yesterday. Today London was blue. Morning dew on the sunflowers by the lock-keeper's cottage glistened. The canal water was yellow green, but clean and clear. I thought about being alone here in England. I thought of China, and my parents. I recalled a strange conversation I had with my mother. It was at my father's graveyard. The thought of how he had lived during his last few weeks made my throat turn to stone.

It was not the Tomb Sweeping season, and we had had my father's burial a few months before. But we were there because I had just received the scholarship to go to Britain, and I had some time to prepare for my departure. I was leaving for good, for a future in the West. There we were, in a large cemetery under a hill with a quarry, on the outskirts of my home town. It was a new cemetery, immense and already crowded. The iron gates were wide enough for four cars to drive through at the same time. We lived in a very populated town, more so than other parts of China. The local government had to cope with the large numbers of the living, but also large numbers of the deceased.

A few months before my father died, my mother had purchased a plot in the cemetery for him. It was only at the burial (not a real burial with a coffin, as the government had banned the practice years ago, but one with an urn) that I discovered that the tomb was so small. It was no more than one square metre. 'It's so expensive, I had to pay the deposit as early as I could.' My mother had told me this in the hospital corridor, even before the doctor announced there was no cure for his cancer. My father didn't know this, of course. None of us would tell him that there was an expensive burial pit waiting for him outside the town.

It was during this second visit to my father's tomb with my mother that I discovered there was a new gravestone erected right next to my father's. The two stones were side by side. The new one had the same style of engraving. My father's headstone had his name and dates of birth and death. That was to be expected. But the writing on the new stone next to his was my mother's name and her birthday. And then a blank space, waiting to be filled. I stood there, astonished, then turned to ask her:

'Why is your gravestone here?'

'Are you stupid?' my mother answered dismissively. She was impatient, as always. She kicked away a little moss-covered rock under her feet, and said: 'You don't know how much they have raised the rent for grave plots, do you? For my spot, I had to pay double what your father's cost! Not to mention the money for the mason! He charged five hundred yuan for that! What a robber! He knows it's a one-off deal!'

She pointed to the space on her headstone, where the death date remained uncarved.

'You will help to add that, won't you?!'

She groaned and brought up a glob of mucus from her throat. She spat it out on the grass beside her shoes. With a clear voice, she added:

'Don't get those thieves to do the job! They don't deserve a penny more.'

I was speechless. My mother had always been a blunt and coarse peasant woman, and I was used to her manners. But I had never imagined that I would have to add the date of her death to her gravestone, with my own hands. Was I meant to carve it with a chisel or screwdriver? It didn't seem real.

Towards the end of this visit, there were almost no words left between us. My mother seemed to have closed herself off in her thoughts. Was she anticipating her own death? In those silent moments, I could not foresee or even have envisaged that my mother would die only a few months later. I knew she had a weak heart, but she was not old, and I didn't expect anything would happen so soon. Out of the blue, she was taken to hospital, after being found unconscious on the ground in our local market. She died of heart failure before I got there. Suddenly, within months, I was an orphan, a grown-up orphan. And all this happened just before I left

China. Were these events signs of my future, condemned to be alone, whether in my native country or abroad?

Before I flew to England, I visited the cemetery one more time. Now my aunt stood beside me, looking at the two gravestones. The date on my mother's remained uncarved. New grass had grown beside my father's. A few daisies. There was still dew on the leaves, shimmering with sunlight. Soon it would evaporate in the midday sun just as we sang that old burial song:

How swiftly it dries, the dew on the garlic-leaf.
The dew that dries so fast.
Tomorrow it will come again.
But he whom we carry to the grave will never return.

Everybody Wants to
Rule the World

– *As Tears for Fears sang:* 'Everybody wants to rule
the world.'
– *Who are these* tears?

Although I had been in Britain for a few months, I still could
not say whether I liked or disliked English people. Somehow,
I had not got to know them. I could not read their emotions.
Some made me feel uneasy, like my professor Grant Stanley. I
feared his cleverness would expose my hidden stupidity.
Something about his way of speaking suggested to me that in
his universe I was a secondary citizen. Maybe also because I
felt that my Western life depended on him, at least my PhD
project. Once I bought a large chocolate bar for him before
our meeting, as I noticed there was always a piece of chocolate
lying around his desk. But when I got to his office, the bar in
my pocket was already melting. I didn't offer it to him. In
Chinese we say 'pat the horse's arse' to mean that you always
offer a little bribe in a relationship. And since the melted chocolate incident, our professional relationship had not been so
good, as if he knew.

Grant had some doubts about my project. 'Project' was an
English word I found impossible to grasp. A vague and
abstract concept. Nevertheless, my *project*, according to the
academic film anthropology style, was a documentary about a

village and its inhabitants in southern China. I had been reading about the village – Jing Cun in Guangdong Province. There were two thousand uneducated workers and peasants living there. But somehow in the last few decades, just about every villager had transformed himself into a painting copyist. They could now reproduce Monet, Chagall and da Vinci at the drop of a hat. I know it's a cliché that almost every Chinese person is a good copyist. But this was still fascinating to me. I could not even draw a proper arm or leg, or paint a tree. Let alone some Western religious figure.

In the corridor I saw my supervisor rushing in my direction. He greeted me and opened his office door, with a mocking exaggeration in his gesture.

'The admin people want to eat me alive! They have left me *no* time to see my students!' Grant pointed to a chair for me. 'Did you read the news this morning about President Xi Jinping's new reforms? He really is trying to be the new Mao!'

'Well. Every leader is an emperor in China, for sure.'

'Yes, as Tears for Fears sang: "*Everybody wants to rule the world.*"'

'Who are these *tears*?' I asked hesitantly. Once again I felt like a fish swimming in a new part of the ocean, unable to recognise the seaweed.

Grant started to hum in a tuneless way, but stopped abruptly. 'Okay, let's get going, no time to lose. Tell me where you are.'

'I've been collecting materials, and made contact with the village. I think I should go there for the actual research and do some filming.'

'That's good to know. Fieldwork is the primary thing in our area.' He then looked at me over his glasses, and added: 'I need to discuss one thing with you before you go further.'

My heart tightened a bit.

'As your supervisor I have an ethical and moral duty to monitor your film-making activities and to ensure that there are no legal complications arising from your filming. It's part of being an anthropologist. So I have some forms for you to fill in. Your secondary supervisor has to sign as well as the head of department.'

He tapped his keyboard and began to print out something.

'What kind of ethical and moral duty?' I asked defensively. 'I thought our purpose was to make a good film *with narrative strength and research value.*' I remembered that this was the phrase he used the other day. 'My film will be quite straightforward. It's just about people in a small village making reproductions of Western art, which they then sell back to the West. What's the issue?'

Grant looked at me with his knitted brow. His hair was a mess, his clothes dishevelled. I wondered if his wife had left him recently.

I stared back at Grant, and didn't feel like talking any more. What did he know about China and Chinese manual workers? Ethical and moral duties? Did he mean that I should get consent forms? Even though Chinese villagers would not give a damn about this sort of formality?

Grant stood up and handed me a dozen printed pages.

'Just fill this in later,' he said, with a slightly impatient tone.

I was about to leave, when Grant suddenly thought of something. He raised his right hand, a Lenin-style gesture, directing me to sit down again.

Authorship

– *But authorship is always an issue.*
– *Didn't Roland Barthes announce the author is dead?*

Grant settled back in his chair, and picked up one of the small figurines from his shelf. It was a dancing tribal woman and he twiddled her in his fingers. He appeared to be reflecting on something we had just discussed. He was breathing in and out heavily. This was usually a sign that he wanted to embark on a more theoretical course of conversation.

'So, I'm curious, you say these workers are originally farmers without any artistic training. How did they learn to draw and to paint? I mean, what is their craftsmanship based on? If a worker makes a hand copy of a Leonardo da Vinci painting, he would need to understand perspective, anatomy, glazing, chiaroscuro and so on.' Grant was on a roll. 'So do they learn simply from copying? But how exactly? Do they learn the skills from their foreman?'

My professor liked to ask questions, but didn't seem to need my answers. He went on:

'You say they are self-taught. Do they have any idea that they have been forging classical artworks and making a profit out of it?'

'No. It is not forging!' I almost laughed. 'These artisans never claim that they are selling the original paintings. They sell reproductions. There is a huge market in the world for them – in hotels, restaurants, people's homes.'

I turned my head, looking around Grant's office. There were no reproductions hanging on his walls here. But I spotted a small postcard of Hockney's *A Bigger Splash* lying by his computer. I pointed to the postcard.

'For example, that is a reproduction, not a forged copy.'

'Yes, I understand. But authorship is always an issue,' Grant claimed.

'Didn't Roland Barthes announce the author is dead? So what the Chinese artisans are enacting is a postmodern phenomenon. They interpret Western paintings with their own eyes and hands.'

'Even if Barthes is right, that does not affect issues of intellectual property rights.'

'Exactly, property rights! What a bourgeois concept!' I found myself speaking like a little Red Guard from Mao's time.

Grant stared at me, with a look of irritation, and said in a slightly clipped tone:

'Okay, it looks like we'll have to agree to disagree.'

I didn't reply. Because I didn't understand what he meant by *we'll have to agree to disagree.*

A Landscape Architect

– But aren't landscape and architecture opposite concepts?
– No. That's like saying love and marriage are opposite
concepts.

The hay fever season continued into the early summer. Everyone in England seemed to be red-eyed and sneezing. It was as if the whole nation was weeping out of some collective grief. The book club met again for the second and last time on a Saturday afternoon. No one wanted to talk about the book we were supposed to discuss this time either. Instead the topic of conversation was the new prime minister, who had come to power after the referendum. I listened with some interest but had nothing to contribute. And I noticed you holding the book but not engaging in the conversation. You were unshaven, but pleasing to the eye.

I turned to you. 'I never asked what you do for your work.'

'I'm a landscape architect.'

Oh. I thought for a moment. This was a new concept for me. I had not met a proper landscape architect before, but plenty of humble gardeners and builders in China. Then, uncertain, I said:

'But aren't landscape and architecture opposite concepts?'

'What do you mean?'

'Architecture is invented by people who want to change the landscape. But landscape doesn't need architects.'

'No.' Your blue-green eyes locked on to me. 'That's like saying love and marriage are opposite concepts.'

Ah. But aren't love and marriage opposite concepts? I wondered. Only fools would get married. Maybe you were a fool, I would find out.

'So tell me, what does a landscape architect do?' I asked.

'Like a gardener, we design outdoor spaces, like community gardens, public parks, children's playgrounds, with details such as where the cars park and where to locate flower beds.'

The women from the reading group were leaving. We stood up, hugging them goodbye. Now only you and I were left on the sofa. You asked:

'So what will you do after finishing your PhD?'

What a question. The British only granted me a three-year visa. And then what? Would I find a job here? Or could I go back to China, with my non-practical qualifications? Should I talk to you about this? I wondered. We didn't know much about each other yet. And, perhaps, you might think I was just like all those Chinese who come here purely with practical aims. Few of them show any imaginative life during their time overseas. That's how Chinese people appear to Western people – in America, in Britain, in Italy, in Spain. Everywhere in the world. Young Chinese students study hard, while old Chinese people work hard. Faceless and voiceless. Should I talk to you about this? Was this a pressing matter for me? The truth was, I had no one to talk to in this country. This was not my country. I knew very few people here.

In the pub, as I was about to reply, a football match started on a giant TV screen above us. Liverpool versus Arsenal? I had thought arsenal was a weapon factory, I didn't know it was a football place too. The noise level became unbearable. I stared at the screen, and thought I could never become an English person. Let alone an English football fan.

爱屋及乌 – *ài wū jí wū*

- *In Chinese we say,* 爱屋及乌 *– ài wū jí wū. Which means if you love your mansion you'll love the magpie too.*
- *Why? What's the connection between mansion and magpie?*
- *In Chinese 'mansion' and 'magpie' have the same pronounciation – wū.*

A room with a view was not my first concern. But a warm bedroom upstairs (no matter how small) with a south-facing window was my basic need in England. After a desperate period of searching, I found a top-floor flat on Richmond Road with two bedrooms. One of the flatmates had decided to go back to Spain. Apparently he was not keen to live in Brexit Britain. The rent was reasonable. I decided I would take it. The other flatmate was a post-doc student, from Italy. She didn't mind the situation in the UK. 'Naples is worse, so I can't complain!' Besides, she was writing a thesis on Swinging Sixties. 'Thank God I got myself out from Naples. I love London. A great city,' she said, while cooking some ravioli in the kitchen.

There was only one bookshelf in the living room. Our books were mixed together. After a few nights, I discovered that she only took my books to read at bedtime, and I, too, took her books to read at night. We both discovered our perfect books to fall asleep with.

Since meeting you, I had bought two books about Germany. One was a history book about Berlin. Another one was *The Magic Mountain*, by Thomas Mann. I was told at university that the magic mountain was a Swiss mountain and not a German one. But it would do for now. I placed the novel on my bedside table, not in the living room. I thought of buying an Australian novel too, perhaps Patrick White's *The Tree of Man*. But maybe I should ask you first.

While I was on the sofa leafing through the Berlin book, my flatmate asked:

'Are you going to Berlin soon?'

'No. But I met a German, actually a half German,' I explained. 'That's why.'

She giggled, and asked: 'And the other half is?'

'Australian,' I answered. 'I know. Opposing characters, like yin and yang.'

'Ha, so you prefer reading books about Germany than Australia?'

Perhaps, I thought. But what do I know about either of these cultures?

'In Chinese we say, 爱屋及乌 – *ài wū jí wū*. Which means if you love your mansion you'll love the magpie too.'

'Why? What's the connection between mansion and magpie?'

'In Chinese "mansion" and "magpie" have the same pronounciation – *wū*.'

She looked at me, as if I had grown three heads. Then she yawned and walked away, carrying her Swinging Sixties book.

On my bed later that evening, in my pyjamas, I looked at Internet images of those ice-age lakes in and around Berlin, and their strange German names: Schlachtensee, Wannsee, Müggelsee, Plötzensee. So they call their lake *see (sea)*. And they call their sea *meer*. Curiously non-English, I thought. This was of course obvious. German is different from English. But still, I realised, I was encountering a third language. This was very different from learning English, because English was always in the atmosphere like pollen from the plants permeating the air, whereas German was like a specific mountain in the landscape which you had to have a particular ambition to climb.

Der Mond – Moon

– Why is moon *masculine in German?*

– There is nothing objective about how you feel *about stars or planets. It's all literature.*

The next time I met you, I asked many questions about your German-ness. Or rather, I interrogated you and even accused you of being Germanic. I found German culture confusing.

'So you are half German. Can I ask you a question? In every culture, *moon* is feminine. In Chinese too. Why is *moon* masculine in German? Do you really see the moon as a male character?'

We were in a Turkish cafe near Dalston. Everyone around us was eating brown mushy chickpeas. People in east London seemed to eat a lot of chickpeas.

'Why is *moon* masculine in German?' You repeated my question.

As if you sensed this was not a simple linguistic question. You thought about it for a few seconds. Then you answered:

'Well, *der Mond*. In some old languages like Sanskrit, the moon is masculine and the sun feminine. I remember learning in school about some pre-Babylonian Sumerian languages, and the word for *moon* is explicitly masculine, as it is in Arabic, in which the word for *sun* is feminine.'

It was like you were giving me a lecture, presenting the findings of some research you had carried out on historical linguistic study.

'I thought you were a landscape architect. But you sound like a linguist. You know a lot about language!'

'A landscape architect knows everything.' You smiled. 'Well, to be honest, this isn't the first time I've been asked this by a non-German speaker.'

'So you think it's just a different tradition that we see the moon as female?'

'Yes, there is nothing objective about how you *feel* about stars or planets. It's all literature. People put too much feeling and emotion into these things.'

I thought about what you said for a while. Perhaps I was just one of those romantic and cultural preservationists who view things according to convention? Or according to the clichés of literature, as you pointed out? But I continued:

'So if *der Stuhl* – the chair – is masculine, then why is the table not feminine? I thought chair and table make a perfect match.'

'There is no logical explanation. There is no why. You just can't ask a question like that about a language.' Your eyes were looking for something, then you pointed to my cutlery. 'For example. You have *die Gabel* – the fork, *der Löffel* – the spoon and *das Messer* – the knife. A fork is feminine, a spoon masculine and a knife neutral. Why? No reason. Just convention. So, the only way to learn the genders of nouns is to treat their articles as a component of the word.'

'That's very unnatural for Chinese people. In our language we don't have articles.'

'You don't have any articles?'

'No. Why bother? We save time for something else.'

'Something else like what?'

'Like enjoying the taste of green tea, or staring into a pond, checking out frogs and lotus flowers.'

You raised your eyebrows, not commenting, but almost laughing. Now the waiter appeared. We began to study the menu, which was full of pictures of all sorts of cooked chickpeas.

'German is a hard language, no?'

'Not as hard as Chinese, probably.' You chuckled. 'I remember when I first came to Germany from Australia. I was in my late teens. One day I learned a word at school: *Geschwindigkeitsbegrenzung*. I got back home and told my father proudly that I'd learned the longest word I'd ever heard. Then he told me that it was the most useless word to learn.'

'*Geschwindig* . . .' I tried to copy this weirdly long word. But I couldn't. You wrote it down on a napkin:

Geschwindigkeitsbegrenzung

'You don't need to remember it, if you don't drive.'

'Do you mind to tell me what it means?'

'Speed limit.'

Ah. I instantly lost interest.

'Do you want to share some chickpeas?' you proposed.

I nodded, tossing the speed limit napkin away.

TWO

南

SOUTH

无语 – *Wu Yu*

> – *I am feeling wordless. I call it* wu yu. *It's like I have lost my language.*
> – *Why lost? If you have really lost one language, aren't you gaining another?*

There had been this feeling of *wu yu* – wordlessness and loss of language – which had enveloped me. It reminded me of something I read in one of Barthes's books. He described how he felt when he visited Japan. The strange signs and sounds. The miscommunication and the silence. The Japan of my world was London, and the strange signs and sounds were from Britain. In my flat, I had not spoken for some days. My flatmate had gone back to Italy to see her family. Four days, alone, in this enclosed place. I listened to the radio, and there seemed to be only two types of news: Brexit and sports. Neither could I connect to, nor could I participate.

It's strange but accurate that English people use the word *flat* to describe a home. *Flat* is a sad concept of *home*. My flat did not feel like a home at all. It was more like a space defined by legal status, where I, as a foreigner, could cook and sleep *legally*. I owned nothing in this country. Come to think of it, I didn't even own myself in this country. My visa, my non-existent income, or my supposed doctor's degree – none of these belonged to me, even though they might temporarily belong to me. Every morning I woke up with anxiety. I made coffee with my flatmate's espresso machine. I chewed anything edible in the kitchen and worked on my thesis till noon.

One day, with an empty stomach, and a doomed feeling about staying in England, I put some rice and water in the rice cooker and plugged it in. I locked the front door and walked to Mare Street to buy groceries. Each time I passed the bus stop, there would be a few Jamaicans or West Indians speaking to each other loudly with their own particular accent. I could not quite follow what they said. Instead I stared at them, like a cold metallic camera. Then there was an ambulance rushing down the road, its siren shrieking. It was so loud that it set off my tinnitus. Before I could escape from the horror of the open-door life, a police car zoomed past, with an even louder siren. Everything seemed to be sending out a message, saying: 'Go home, jobless people. Go home, foreigners. Go home, losers.'

I walked back to my flat and cooked some minced tofu. There was no soy sauce left, but I found a bottle of brown sauce. I opened the bottle and sniffed, without knowing what was in it. I poured some onto my tofu. I thought the white bean curd needed some dark sauce. I tried a little. It tasted awful. Really awful! I spat out the strange-flavoured tofu and looked at the label on the bottle. It said that it was based on the famous Worcestershire Sauce. But what was Worcestershire? A province in England? A rainy place with some cows wandering around? Do the locals produce special herbs for Brown Sauce? Did this sauce distil the essence of the place? Would I ever visit there?

In the afternoon, I read books related to my study. I felt aches growing stronger in my back and neck. My throat was dry. And I needed to go out. Perhaps, I should talk to people, speak in some language, any language, and hear the language of others too. Any language.

In the evening, I was thinking about calling you. But I didn't. I didn't want to make you think that I was a needy person. I thought I should walk to the canal, to my lock-keeper's cottage. But I was a little afraid of dark. So instead, I wrote to you:

'I am feeling wordless. I call it *wu yu*. It's like I have lost my language.'

You wrote back:

'Why lost? If you have really lost one language, aren't you gaining another?'

I read your words a few times. I thought, why can't I hold on to one language while gaining another at the same time? Why do I have to lose one first? I looked out into the dull night sky, and got no answer.

Vibrations

– We could play in a band together. I feel there are musical vibrations between us.
– Vibrations?

You told me you had always lived in this part of London since moving here several years ago. You said you 'love' this area. *Love* – a strong word, I thought. But maybe you meant you 'really like' the area.

We were in Kingsland Road. It looked nothing like a *King's Land* should be. Nor did I understand its 'trendyness'. For people like me from China or other countries that have only recently escaped poverty, the sight of poor people barging into each other in a chaotic market with rats running around and fish rotting on the pavement was not that 'trendy'.

'At least our two countries have something in common when it comes to naming streets.' I looked at the road signs around me.

'Really? Tell me.'

'In China, we name streets with upbeat Communist concepts. For example, New China Road, Army-Worker Avenue, Deng Xiaoping Pathway, May First Drive . . . and in Britain you have Tudor Road, Kingsland Road, Victoria Park, Queensgate, Knightsbridge . . .'

You laughed.

'I don't understand why people think propaganda is a Chinese thing – what's the difference here?' I muttered, with some bitterness.

'Well, there are some differences between communism and feudalism.'

'If so, at least we are more advanced than you guys.' Then I remembered something: 'Especially that Olympic park. What is it called again? Queen Elizabeth's Park! What did she contribute to it? I bet her feet never landed on that part of the world.'

'You're right, England has never been a modern country.' You guided me through the busy street. 'My house will be a good example.'

We came to a side street where your *house* was. Your house? You mean *a real house*? A *fangzi*? I wondered to myself.

We stopped before a dilapidated factory building with rusty pipes everywhere forming a giant spiderweb on the wall. You brought me into a dark and narrow staircase that led to your flat.

You told me you shared the flat with a musician. 'That's why all these instruments,' you explained, and seemed to be embarrassed. 'Sorry for the mess.'

It was a bachelor's home. No doubt. Oily plates and dirty cups filled the sink. Big leather boots here and there. On the dining table, there was a heavy picture book, entitled *Brutalist London*. Then another big photo book about Frank Gehry. By the sofa, there were two guitars and a small ukulele with loose strings. Why a ukulele? This instrument was normally played by a woman, or a hippy, or a Polynesian prince. At least that's what we Chinese thought.

'Do you play the ukulele?' I asked, plucking the strings. It was out of tune.

'Not much. But guitar, yes.'

You began to tidy up, putting the guitars away so I could sit on the sofa. It felt to me like you rarely had visitors here. Your gestures were clumsy, and I didn't think you had ever tried to clean up your place before.

While you were making me some tea, I fiddled with the broken ukulele. I learned to play when I was in college. I thought four strings were easier to handle than six. And I always loved the small shape of a ukulele. I found the instrument beautiful.

'You play well!' You brought me the tea. 'Even with a missing string!'

With the three strings, I tried the only part I could remember from 'Raindrops Keep Falling on My Head':

Raindrops keep falling on my head
But that doesn't mean my eyes will soon be turning red
Crying's not for me
'Cause I'm never gonna stop the rain by complaining
Because I'm free . . .

I stopped. A little abashed, I said: 'I have not played it for so many years. My fingers are stiff.'

'I like it.' You sat close to me on the sofa. 'I should buy some strings.' Then you looked at me, and spoke almost teasingly: 'We can play in a band together. I feel there are some musical vibrations between us.'

'Vibrations?' I laughed. How was I meant to respond to these words?

Suddenly we both became quiet and felt tense. Then one of us bumped into the ukulele and it fell to the floor. You picked it up, laid it carefully against the bookshelf.

When does a physical relationship begin? Is it when the lovers kiss or when they imagine their kissing beforehand? Is it when their eyes meet and knowingly gaze at each other? We kissed. That's how I date the beginning of our physical relationship.

Penetrative Sex vs Non-penetrative Sex

– I don't know if I like penetrative sex.
– What do you mean?
– I prefer non-penetrative sex. I prefer kissing, tenderness and our bodies being close.

From early July, the city totally changed its appearance. The sun decided to stay up in the sky for as long as it could, and its golden rays pierced down and made my body warm. Giant hydrangeas bloomed in front of the once grey council buildings. London planes stretched out their tough branches and hard leaves onto the summery air.

It happened very fast. I stayed in your flat for the following week, almost every night. The outside world disappeared. There was only you and me. Our bodies parted for some hours during the day, but we found ourselves in each other's arms again in the evening. How I loved the way you enveloped me, one arm around my neck and shoulders, and the other holding my hip. Our legs entwined. My long hair covered my face whenever you kissed me, as if it were a veil to keep you from seeing and feeling me clearly.

'Should I shave my head?' I asked, half joking, while trying to pull back strands of my hair.

'No, it's so lovely,' you said with seriousness.

You entered me. You filled me completely. My womb contracted. It felt like my body was bursting. But I held on to you, and wouldn't let you come.

'I can hardly take being inside you,' you whispered, trembling slightly.

'What do you mean?'

'It's too much. I can barely stop myself coming.'

You stopped speaking, as if you were in some sweet pain. We both breathed in and out, and felt the same force travelling between us. No. There was no *us*, but one form.

After that, we rested in bed, letting the sweat dry on the sheets. My head was buried in your chest. We didn't talk for a while. You were thinking about something, something I could not guess or understand. Your eyes were now lingering on the light coming from the window. They were no longer on me. I didn't like their absence. I felt you had moved away from me, as least your mind had, along with its elusive thoughts. Then into the silence, I said:

'I don't know if I like penetrative sex.'

'What do you mean?'

'I prefer non-penetrative sex. I prefer kissing, tenderness and our bodies being close.'

'So you don't like it when I'm inside you?' You raised your upper body, supporting yourself with an arm and now stared at me.

'When you're inside me, it's like you're intruding, forcefully. I can't then *feel* love any more.'

'What do you mean you can't feel love any more? Surely you are taking me into you. Isn't that an act of love?'

'But it's not you. It's just your penis.'

'Yes, but in that moment, we are both so absorbed in our bodies, in that pleasure. So, it's not just my penis. It's me, and it's you, taking me in!'

'Not for me. I'm not focused on my vagina. I'm in my whole body. It's the man who treats his penis as himself. Like an instrument.'

You said nothing. Were you offended? But I could not deny my feelings. After penetrative sex I felt lonely, and a little empty. Perhaps that's because I did not connect with this idea of penetration. The idea that you filling my vagina with your penis would complete me emotionally. It did not. And once you were out, my incompleteness came back to me even more powerfully and I felt I was alone, all alone. What took away my sense of incompleteness was our bodies being entwined, the barriers of our skins falling away. That wasn't about penetration at all. But that did not seem to be how it was for you.

After another week I felt we had calmed down a bit. Our bodies were less hungry for each other. Every morning we had breakfast together, then you left for work. I would leave your place and walk back to my flat. I studied and wrote for the rest of the day. When the evening light descended on the oak trees outside the window, I began to feel unloved and was longing to see you again. I always hoped you would jump on an earlier train to come back. But you rarely did. On the contrary, you often came back later than I expected.

After dusk, I walked back to your flat, feeling anxious. The days were still long as the summer grew older. I watched people going home with their shopping bags, their children following behind. The rows of houses from my flat to yours were concrete grey council houses – the kind I would not regard as *nice*, as the English would say. The iron fences were high, and the security cameras hovered like aliens above each street corner. London was the most fenced city I had ever seen or lived in. But at least these ugly council houses were home for the ordinary families who lived there. I didn't even have an ugly home. Under the white street light I felt weightless and deserted. Was it about our relationship? Or was it a deeper anxiety about my own future? I refrained from indulging in my disturbing thoughts. I walked towards your place as my temporary fix, a powerful distraction. Love makes people blind. But how I desperately needed this blindness, at least for now.

Our lovemaking continued with penetration. Why? Was it because that's what men and women do when they are in love? Was I submitting myself to you because I feared I might lose you?

Elderflower Lemonade

– *When I was a kid I'd go out into the fields and collect shoots and then cook them at home.*

– *Ha! When I was a kid in Australia I'd go out, chop down shrubs, chase lizards and throw stones at sparrows. But we never ate shoots. We'd just go to the supermarket.*

One afternoon, after another morning in bed, we went for a long walk. We walked all the way along the Hackney Marsh. By the River Lea, there were large patches of elderflower bushes. So abundant, despite being late in the season. You could not help but start to pick them. I watched you, remembering how I first met you. The elderflower picker. I found that really special, even though now I knew you much better and you were less enigmatic than before. Then I followed you, uprooting the flowers one by one. I found myself returning to my childhood, with you.

'When I was a kid I'd go out into the fields and collect shoots and then cook them at home.'

'Ha! When I was a kid in Australia I'd go out, chop down shrubs, chase lizards and throw stones at sparrows. But we never ate shoots. We'd just go to the supermarket.'

We brought a big bunch back home. The tough stems made my cheeks and hands itchy.

You showed me how to make elderflower lemonade.

'The thing about making elderflower lemonade is that it makes you want to return to nature again. It's a strange effect. Almost like addiction.'

Almost like addiction – I repeated this in my heart. Right now, my addiction was you, your body. Your caress. Your kiss. You inside me. I would not tell you again I preferred non-penetrative sex. I liked both. I also liked our lives whether we were having sex or not. Sex was always there, like a secret fragrance, even when we did ordinary things together, like crushing elderflowers.

When you were cooking elders, you were like a scientist doing an experiment. You were not distracted by me. You taught me how to boil up the cordial. We heated a pot of sugar syrup first, then cut the flower heads off the stems. You opened the boiling pot and instructed me:

'The flowers should be steeped in the water!'

Steeped in the water? I asked myself. I knew I should put the heads in the pot, but I didn't know what '*steeped in*' was. I didn't want to look stupid, so I vaguely dipped the flower heads in the boiling water, remembering the very first conversation when we met.

You watched over my shoulder and I could feel your breath on my skin. You added lime and lemon juice.

'The acid will help preserve the cordial and add tartness.'

Hmm, tartness. A new word. A nuanced word. I liked learning words from you.

I dipped my spoon into the liquid and tasted the syrup. It was thickly sweet and sour. Too sour, actually, but I liked having the experience.

'Are you sure you are making the right drink?' I wheezed. 'This tastes like the cough medicine we drink in China.'

You laughed and took back my spoon. 'Normally we don't drink it directly. You always add water to dilute it before you drink.'

Oh. I swallowed the last drop of sugary water on the back of my tongue and said nothing.

You poured a little of the syrup into a glass and mixed it with sparkling water.

'Try this now.'

I tried. Yes, it tasted so much better. It was delicious.

You stored the liquid in two bottles and put them in the fridge. Now we sat down at the kitchen table, both looking at those headless green stems. Without the flowers, they looked like a particular type of weed we would feed to pigs in China: 猪草 – pig weeds.

Our life with your flatmates was an odd one. They were like strangers yet friendly, and so close to us physically. We wondered if they could hear us in bed. We could not hear them, so we pondered if they made love at all. One night I heard a cry. Was it pleasure or a bad dream? I would look into the Irish girl's eyes in the morning to discern some truth of her love life at night. But I found no clue. I could feel the warmth of her body as I squeezed past her in the kitchen, and thought of her boyfriend touching her.

Art for Art's Sake

*— Mao said there is no such thing as art for art's sake, art
that stands above classes, art that is detached from or
independent of politics.*

— On that note I agree with Mao.

As I originally thought about it, doing a PhD was a way of
finding a place in the real world – with a set of 'specialist'
vocabularies and methods I would have more chance to compete. But I didn't find myself engaged in most of my seminars,
nor was I inspired by talking to my supervisor. Why was that?
I asked myself. Perhaps I didn't find anything real in that environment. For me, the conflicts and discussions worth being
part of were coming from the everyday world, not from aca-
demia. Sitting in lecture theatres just made me feel, acutely, a
disconnection from life.

I returned home late one night, and told you about a
meeting with Professor Grant. I said I would go to China in
less than a year for my film project.

'Did he agree with your proposal and everything?' you
asked.

'More or less. We talked about the Walter Benjamin essay –
"The Work of Art in the Age of Mechanical Reproduction".'

'Oh, how come?'

'Because it is related to my research.'

'But *mechanical reproduction* is to do with machines – you said the Chinese workers reproduce paintings with their hands. It's not quite the same thing, is it?'

'Oh, please don't take it so literally. You're like my professor! Overly pedantic and a bit picky.' I was impatient. I couldn't attack my professor, but I could attack you. So I continued: 'Don't you see my Chinese artisans are acting like machines?! They are reproducing machine-like behaviour.'

'Okay, but isn't that quite a negative, dehumanising perspective on humans?'

'It is, and it isn't. They are machine-like. Andy Warhol said he wanted to be a machine. It can be quite liberating too. Individual thought is overly worshipped, don't you think?'

I paused, realising all this was actually not relevant. The mere fact of those workers selling their reproductions to anyone who could afford them, so the lower classes could enjoy some level of art too, was simply a good thing.

'Mao said in his *Little Red Book*: *There is no such thing as art for art's sake, art that stands above classes, art that is detached from or independent of politics.*'

'Hmm, on that note I agree with Mao.'

You then added:

'Take Bauhaus. I am German enough to like the Bauhaus. Those guys saw no separation between art and social conditions. The aesthetic was the functional. Buildings were machines for living.'

'But I really hate Bauhaus. They either look like bunkers or containers!' I snapped. 'In China, we have Bauhaus everywhere – from big cities to small villages. Gigantic, grey, cold, and all looking the same. No one would call that art. I wish they could be blown up.'

I opened and closed your fridge – there was nothing in it, just a bare space that reminded me of some ugly modernist construction.

You got up from your chair, looking a little peeved. You never wanted to spend too much time on an intellectual discussion. You were a man interested in physical reality. Sometimes you preferred to stare at a tree rather than talk about culture.

A bit later, after we had finished our supper and I had calmed down, you asked:

'Why don't you tell your flatmate that you are moving out in a month and living with me?'

I looked at you, nodded. I found myself having the thought: we are becoming a real couple. Then I was wondering what that meant. I heard people using these words, but where would it take us?

Living-boat

– I would love to live on a boat . . .
– Seriously? On a boat?

We didn't ask your flatmate for permission for me to move in.
You said it wasn't an issue. The landlord would not know how
many people were living in the house, and besides, your flatmate's girlfriend also stayed here without paying extra rent.
We could all live together with very little cost.

Now we four people shared a two-bedroom flat with a tiny
bathroom. The toilet was always busy and the kitchen was
always full of steamy pots and the smell of fried onions. In the
bedroom, we turned on Radio 3 all day long so we didn't have
to listen to the music from the next room. I had never listened
to so much classical music in my life – now Radio 3 had fixed
a station somewhere in my brain. And it would play on its
own even when I unplugged the radio.

In the evening, after everyone returned from work, we
either hid in our bedroom, or went out for a walk till the flatmates had finished eating. One night not long after I'd moved
in, you told me you wanted to move out.

'Yes. I agree. This is like living in a Chinese dormitory!' I
said.

'I would love to live on a boat,' you murmured.

'Seriously? On a boat?'

'Yes. One of those narrowboats you see on the canal.'

This was completely out of blue. Even though I'd noticed you always slowed down whenever we walked along Regent's Canal, I had not realised you were looking at boats and imagining a life on them. We often walked from Victoria Park, along the water, towards Dalston, and you would stop by the canal watching people moor and ask them about their firewood and stoves.

You gazed wistfully out through the window. There were grim-looking estates, treeless backyards littered with rubbish. You said, slightly dispirited:

'When I studied architecture at Edinburgh, we looked at Frank Gehry and some other architects' designs. I often asked myself: would I be happy to live in those buildings for the rest of my life? Deep down I'm ambivalent. I find those designs too crude. Those monuments were born from the ego, but not for people. I would rather live in a tree house, or on a boat, if I could.'

This was the first time I learned that you had doubts about what you had studied and devoted your life to.

'But don't you like your profession?'

'Yes, I love my work. But at the Design School it was all about selling your ideas, no matter how unsuitable they might be in reality. That's why I preferred landscape design, which is not so much focused on buildings but more to do with the environment and nature.'

'What about Edinburgh? You studied there for a few years. Isn't it a nice city to live in?'

'Yes, but as a modern architect, what was I supposed to do in an all-listed old town? We couldn't touch anything, every building and every stone was protected. There was no space to experiment.'

I see. Now I understood you a little more, I thought. Especially the way you see a perfect space to live in. But on a boat? In a city like London? I was not convinced.

'I like the Regent's Canal,' you said. 'It has both a natural and an industrial feel. There is a particular English charm.'

'But where on the canal? It is a long canal, going through the whole city!'

'Anywhere. We can find a quiet spot by the park or near some woods.'

You paused, distracted by the sound of repeated flushing from the bathroom. The toilet always needed some encouragement. We often had to pour water from a bucket into the bowl.

You tried to ignore the sound of toilet activities and continued: 'On a boat, we won't have to share our kitchen or bathroom any more.'

I liked that idea. I imagined drinking morning coffee half naked on a boat, or reading a novel by the water and looking at ducks drifting by.

'But I know nothing about driving a boat, let alone how to maintain one.' I started to panic. 'I don't even know where the engine is, or which direction is the front or back!'

'You'll learn. If you can write an 80,000-word PhD thesis, then you can learn to drive a boat!'

Really? I knew some professors who could write multiple volumes of history but didn't know how to use a rice cooker, or fix a bike. Before I could express my doubt, you opened your laptop and began to search boat-renting websites.

I thought of my favourite place. The mournful but peaceful spot by the canal. The lock-keeper's cottage. That would be somewhere I would like to live, if I had to choose between a boat and a house. I was not sure how I would feel, if the ground beneath my feet swayed a little every day.

Mooring

– *Aren't you worried about having to change mooring all the time?*

– *Not really, you are my mooring.*

During the next few weeks we spent time looking for a boat to rent or buy. We even took a train to the north of England to see two boats for sale. They were not expensive but the question was how we could bring one back to London. It would take weeks, crossing towns and different waterways. What if we got stuck somewhere? Then we found another boat. It was in Essex. We went down there. The boat owner said he would give us a good deal if we could bring it to London by ourselves. We hesitated. What about your work and my time? We would need a two-week holiday for this job. We were pathetic! We could not even manage two weeks – unless we waited till Christmas and the New Year break.

Eventually, we found a small boat for sale in Berkshire. It was a black semi-trad, and the price was affordable. We instantly decided to put all our money together to buy it. It was scary. I kept looking into your eyes after we made the decision. And I asked myself again and again, are you sure? This was the biggest decision I had made since coming to Britain. Perhaps no decision in the end is right or wrong. All decisions are just decisions. They are just taking one more step in the garden of forking paths – they lead to the same place in the end.

The boat was moored in Purley on Thames, an old and dispiriting spot near Reading. And we had to bring it back to wherever we wanted to live. Well, we didn't know where we could moor it yet, but at least we could bring it back to London, somewhere on the Regent's Canal.

How difficult would it be to get the mooring licence for living boats in London? And would it be safe? Before signing the contract, I researched a bit online and these things worried me. You were about to send the money to the boatman. I stopped you and asked:

'Aren't you worried about having to change the mooring all the time?'

And here was your answer: 'Not really, you are my mooring.'

I laughed and you smirked. Then I thought. My vanity of wanting a so-called 'romantic' life repelled all the practical concerns. So we signed the contract. After that we received two rusty keys. Too late now – we'd bought the shabby little boat with a broken ceiling and crooked deck.

'I'll fix it once we get back to London,' you promised me confidently. And you wanted to make love right away, in our hotel, somewhere by the Thames near Reading.

She

– She is lovely.

– Why do you call a boat a she and not a he? For me, a boat is male. It drifts. What else could it be?

The boat had a name, painted on the side: *Old Mary*. A sad name to my ears. So we gave it a new name – *Misty*. Even though to sail through a mist was not a good idea for a boat. And it would take us a few more weeks to put a new coat of paint on it and a new name plaque on the side. From the moment our feet landed on *Misty*, we occupied ourselves with physical work. And we were stuck in Purley on Thames for a week before the boat could be moved through the water.

You had this visible joyfulness as soon as you got on board. You touched every single piece of wood or metal on the boat as if they were part of your body, your skin. As for me, I didn't really know how to describe my feelings. Because on the one hand, living on a boat was like not having a home any more. No roots, no land. I was deserting the solid earth, because of you, and launching myself onto an unstable surface. On the other hand I knew that I had started a different life here, with you, away from my Chinese roots, away from a formulated city life. But a feeling of panic got hold of me. I felt I was neglecting my PhD studies because of this boat. Our days were completely taken up with *Misty* now. You never walked around without a tool in your hand: hammer, nail, screwdriver, boards, ladder. And every day I wrote a long to-do list. These were the daily tasks I had to achieve in my new life:

1. Throw away my high heels and wear only practical boots or trainers.
2. Empty a pump-out toilet system regularly, moving the dirty water tank under the plastic 'bathroom'.
3. Always keep an eye on the sink and toilet to avoid the moment that the boat becomes a poo-floating space.
4. Manage a temperamental heavy fuel stove and live with running out of gas at midnight.
5. Wonder what that strange noise from the engine or the bilges might be, and worry about security on the towpath and whether your bike is still on the roof . . .

This was the new mode of my life now. I rose early. And I no longer spent time looking at myself in the mirror or showering in the mornings. There was no mirror on the boat, and the shower was broken. Everything was about the practicalities, like getting my fingers dirty and my thumbs oily. If my parents were still alive, I wondered how they would react to my life in Britain. And if they would come all the way to 'rescue' me from this insanity as they would have viewed it. There must be some positive aspects to one's parents passing away. Now I was free to be insane, or stupid. And I had to see my current life as one of the positive things I had gained from losing my former Chinese life.

When *Misty* finally had a new coat of paint, the boat looked very shiny, almost grand and pompous. You jumped onto the pavement by the canal and inspected it from the distance. You said:

'She is lovely.'

I thought you were talking about a woman who was passing by. When I realised you meant the boat, I was annoyed.

'Why do you call a boat a *she* and not a *he*?' I protested. 'For me, a boat is male. It drifts. What else could it be?'

You shrugged your shoulders. 'Women drift too, don't you think?'

I didn't know what to say about that. I would find out, I thought, when I grew a bit older.

Spüren – Feel

– Now I can feel *life. In German* feel *is* spüren. *I prefer* spüren, *somehow.*
– Spüren *sounds much heavier than* feel.

We spent much less time on our computers now. I had put aside my writing and film research, and was now concerned only with our life afloat. This canal was two hundred years old. It was not that old compared with the Grand Canal in China, which was built 2,400 years ago. But I felt this one had a much older texture than the one in my country. I could not explain why – perhaps the whole atmosphere? The decayed banks, the moss-entangled water, and the views of relics and wrecks along the waterway. What was the purpose of our adventure, though? No great purpose, no kings or queens or new lands awaited us. To live on the boat itself was the purpose, as you said.

'Now I can *feel* life,' you announced, with a heavy accent on *feel*. 'In German *feel* is *spüren*. I prefer *spüren*, somehow.'

'*Spüren* sounds much heavier than *feel*,' I responded. 'It's like you prefer black rye bread to the soft dough.'

My life was much more physical than it used to be. I felt (*Ich spürte*) I was some nameless peasant wife again. But why *again*? I asked myself. I had never been a wife before, but I did feel being a wife was a very familiar role. As if I had played that role many times and I knew exactly what I was supposed to do. Instead of reading and writing, or thinking about my project, all the time I worried about basic things – filling up the water container, checking the gas bottles. I would never just take a walk for the pleasure of it. I would carry either rubbish bags or a huge water bottle for ten minutes until a public bin or a fountain appeared, or endlessly charge batteries for various electrical equipment on the boat.

The weather was still decent enough for us to eat outside. Occasionally it was cold at night, especially when it rained. But it was still *lovely* – a word used often in England when talking about something that is nice. You didn't use this word, I noticed, you used this other word: *comfortable*.

You didn't work this week. You said you were taking a few days off so you could repair the boat. You climbed up, nailing the last piece of wooden board onto the new roof. From now on, with the new roof, at least we would not get rained on. Now you were adding a layer of *felt*. But this *felt* was not *spürte*. It was a waterproof material made from wool which would protect our little roof under the wet sky.

西厢 *Xixiang – Western Chamber*

- *Now I feel I'm one of those young ladies in ancient Chinese literature, who live in a Xixiang, and look out of the west window for the views of willows and sparrows, waiting for their man to return.*
- *Except that your man has nowhere to return from. He doesn't want to be anywhere but here!*

The head of the boat faced east, the tail west. The main room was just the central part of *Misty*, with the door opening to the eastern sun. I called this part that served as lounge and kitchen the Eastern Chamber. Our bedroom was built in the tail. I called it Western Chamber, as it faced the setting sun. In my Western Chamber, I read on my bed and slept, with the views of willow branches dipping into the canal water. Now I realised that I was indeed living in a Xixiang – the Western Chamber – which had been the symbolic position of Chinese girls' lives in our ancient romantic tales. And you, the man, stayed in Dongxiang – the Eastern Chamber – fixing things and making a noise.

'Have you heard of the Chinese classic called *Xixiang Ji – Romance of the Western Chamber?*'

The boat was small enough that we could talk to each other from either side.

'It was written seven hundred years ago, during the Yuan Dynasty. Our equivalent of *Romeo and Juliet*. It's about a young woman's secret love affair with a man. She lives in a Xixiang – a Western Chamber – and the man has to read poems and sing every day discreetly under her window, so her parents won't find out.'

You smiled, and asked: 'Do they manage to be together in the end? Or do the parents find out and separate them?'

'Ah, depends which version of the play you read, or watch. There are many different versions. But the most popular one has a happy ending.'

You nodded. Then you moved between the Eastern Chamber and Western Chamber, with an electric drill in your hand.

'Now I feel I'm one of those young ladies in ancient Chinese literature who live in a Xixiang, and look out of the west window for the views of willows and sparrows, waiting for their man to return.'

'Except that your man had nowhere to return from. He doesn't want to be anywhere but here!'

Your voice was muffled by the drilling noise. You had designed a mini kitchen a few days ago, with an unusual curve to fit the shape of the boat. And now you wanted to install an asymmetrical cupboard. I was looking forward to it. Once we had a mini kitchen then I could at least avoid stacking our plates and cooking pots on the floor of the Eastern Chamber.

Later on, rain started to fall. The canal water became dark, with millions of small ripples dancing about. The ripples were everywhere outside my west window. I thought of a poem by a Tang Dynasty poet, Li Shangyin. It was entitled 'Ye Yu Ji Bei' – 'Night Rains, Greet the North'. The lines went:

You ask when I'll be back but there is no when
Night rains are flooding autumn ponds in the mountain
Indeed when will we sit together again and trim the wicks in
  the west window,
And talk about Ba Mountain and night rains?

It's about leaving, and not returning. But why did I keep thinking about leaving? Was it the fear that you would leave me one day? Or was it the despondent feeling of my having left China for the West? Through my west window, I could see the rain was receding. The canal was illuminated by the lamps lit here and there along the bank.

家 jiā – Home

– *Why is it that the character for* home *is a pig in a house rather than a person in a house?*

– *Because in the old days, pigs were counted as people in the household registration.*

Now we had a *home* for ourselves. A little roof under the sky. *Misty.* It belonged to you and me. A home, a *jiā*. I thought of a pig under the roof. The Chinese character 家 (*jiā*) consists of two radicals. One is 豕 – a symbol for pig. The other is 宀 – a symbol for roof.

'Why is it that the character for *home* is a pig in a house rather than a person in a house?' you asked.

'Because in the old days, pigs were counted as people in the household registration,' I explained. 'A house with people in it doesn't mean it is resourceful. But a house with a pig in it suggests that a family is self-sufficient and wealthy.'

You thought about what I said. Not entirely convinced, you asked: 'But I often see they hang a pig's head in Chinese restaurants or in a kitchen. It's not the prettiest of pictures with flies all over its skin. Is that a symbol of a good kitchen?'

'Why not? I don't see the contradiction in this. It's about how we can feed ourselves.' Then I added: 'Maybe your family never needed to worry about feeding itself?'

You looked at me, in silence. You began to prepare supper. You told me you would make a German dish tonight – *Kartoffelsalat*. Even though I told you I hated eating cold food, and I did not like stuffing myself with potatoes. But you didn't care. *Kartoffelsalat*, that's what you decided to make. Potato and black bread – a sorrowful view in a Chinese kitchen. My tongue would need some stimulation to get through a night of boiled potatoes.

更 – *Geng*

  – *We should make a geng-clock, instead of having an*
    hour-clock. Counting hours is not useful on the boat.
  – *I like this geng-clock idea.*

Time felt different living on the water.

In Chinese tradition, a geng is about two and a half hours, which is exactly how my sleep cycle was on the boat. I woke up almost every geng. In the beginning, if I woke up in the dark, I couldn't immediately work out where I was. It would take a while to realise that I was not sleeping in a flat – in a bedroom with four walls. Then I became fully awake and would visualise the shape of the boat, and the orientation of the windows. There was only a tiny window by the bed, and it was high up to avoid water. The bed was not rectangular but had an elongated and round-cornered structure. And you were beside me, warm and sleeping soundly. You didn't have the habit of waking up at *the third geng*.

Then I thought that it was more appropriate for boat life to be measured by gengs instead of by hours. And after listening to the sound of water, I fell asleep again with the gentle swing of the boat – if there was a wind.

In the morning after you woke up, I half joked:

'We should make a geng-clock, instead of having an hour-clock. Counting hours is not useful on a boat.'

'I like the geng-clock idea. Maybe I can make this machine, and sell it to the world and we'll be very rich.'

I smiled. But who would buy them? A hippy community? Certainly not people who do banking and financing – they would need a minute-clock not a slow geng-clock.

Horny

– You look like you want to say something to me.
– Well, yes . . . I was feeling very horny this morning.

Today after a cold sandwich lunch (another cold lunch!) on the deck, I decided to plant some coriander and chives. I had collected a few abandoned wooden boxes, but I needed soil. When I got back from the park with bags of soil, you were eating the last packet of oatcakes.

'Caught you!' I yelled. 'Go and buy some more! I am not going to the shop again today!'

The supermarket was far from our mooring location. It was you who insisted on mooring the boat in such an isolated area, because of its 'peace and quiet'. I resented that. All I wanted for my foreigner's life was to live in the most central area where I could see life and action right in front of me.

Apologetically, you paced up and down in our cramped Eastern Chamber, wondering whether to make another cup of coffee. I said:

'Let's go to a cafe, so we don't waste gas.'

'Six pounds for two coffees. With that money we could buy a small bottle of gas.'

I nodded, watching you making coffee. Then you moved around swiftly with some tools in your hands, checking here and there. Wearing only a pair of shorts, you looked healthy and sexy. This floating life suited you perfectly.

Then I remembered something I was going to tell you that morning, but I hadn't found the right time to say it.

'You look like you want to say something to me.'

'Well, yes . . . I was feeling very *horny* this morning.'

'Really? When?'

'When I was still asleep, and you were sleeping. It was early. I was in a loop of sexual dreams, or maybe a lucid dream of wanting to have sex.'

'Hmm.' You listened with interest and poured some coffee into my cup. 'Why didn't you wake me up?'

'I was too sleepy. But as soon as I got up, the practicalities took over, and I forgot about it.'

'Then why don't we do it now?' You drank your coffee, and put down the cup.

'Now?' I looked at you, amused. 'But we are busy, no time.'

'Come here. It's warmer . . .'

Once we got onto the bed, I no longer felt horny. The bed was cold, the duvet heavy. I was distracted by a patch of bird poo, dried on the bedside window. But we made love.

Barthesian Love Discourse 1

— No female point of view at all. But still, women like the book.

What did Barthes know about love? Even though I was the one who really loved his *A Lover's Discourse: Fragments*, I didn't know anything about this French author's emotional life. Actually, you were the one who knew more about his personal life.

'Roland Barthes was homosexual. He never dated a woman in his life,' you told me in one of those bedtime reading hours. Those hours were always the best time to conduct an interesting conversation.

'Really? But it cannot be true!' I reacted with exasperation. I always thought someone like Barthes must have been a typical Frenchman with multiple romantic relationships with bohemian ladies.

'You never noticed that he barely mentions women in his books? Especially in *A Lover's Discourse?*'

'Oh.' I tried to recall what I had read some years ago. 'Hmm, I never thought about this.'

'The only woman he wrote about was his mother. And she was the only woman he lived with in his entire life.'

I was very surprised. I looked at you suspiciously. How could a landscape architect know so much about Roland Barthes's life?

'It's not that mysterious. I studied Barthes at university, and read a biography about him. I also read biographies of Nietzsche and Kaiser Friedrich II, if you're interested.'

I didn't quite know who Kaiser Friedrich II was, but I wouldn't ask now.

You went on: 'Barthes's father was killed during World War I. So he grew up with his mother and lived with her for sixty years, until the day she died. He had a few erotic encounters with boys in Morocco. But that was all.'

I went silent.

For me, Barthes's discourses on love represented the complex relations between a man and a woman. I had always thought of it as heterosexual love. Now you told me this love expert had never really been romantically involved with any woman. Everyone, including me, believed the book had been about two points of view – man/woman and woman/man thinking about each other and reflecting on their desire. I had always identified myself with the supposed woman in the discourse. But in fact the book was a homosexual man's view about love and desire. There was no discourse, at least no dialogue between men and women. Nor was there between men and men. It was like a solipsistic monologue.

For all these years, the book had been a personal document for me, speaking to me. But now I had to admit it wasn't speaking to me, or of me, exactly. Or not in the way I thought it had. What should I make of it after this?

'No female point of view at all,' you said. 'But still, women like the book.'

Putting down a photographic book about landscape designs in Colorado, you got up and went to the front deck.

The boat was swinging very slightly in the water. I liked these floating moments, feeling the wind and the water around us. It was never static like living in a concrete house. But still, if what you said was true, would I still like the book as much as I used to? Did I feel cheated? For a woman like me, love was romantic first, then it grew domestic, and then it became concrete and there would be no room for an ungrounded play of romance.

Had I completely misunderstood Barthes?

Or had I misunderstood myself?

Barthesian Love Discourse 2

– *I know it's a different kind of love. But even if Barthes
had loved some men, it would be nothing compared to
his love for his mother, right?*
– *Yes. But it's more this: any romantic love would not be
able to gain space if the person were totally tied to his
maternal love.*

So for the next few days, I sat in a cafe near the boat and read
about Barthes's life. I found out more. A contradictory figure.
In the daytime Barthes was an orderly Protestant who wrote
and worked, but at night he would abandon himself in Parisian
gay bars. He was a champion of hedonism who never publicly
proclaimed his homosexuality. Certainly he was not a figure
like Pier Paolo Passolini or Rainer Werner Fassbinder, who
had fearless lives when it came to their homosexuality. So was
Barthes totally bourgeois and willing to live in hypocrisy, a
double life, because of cowardice?

And then there was his mother. The only constant love in
his life was the love for his mother. I read a paragraph from his
diary *Journal de Deuil*:

The awesome but not painful idea that she (mother) had
not been everything to me. Otherwise I would never have
written any work. Since my taking care of her for six

months long, she actually had become everything for me, and I totally forgot ever having written anything at all. I was nothing more than hopelessly hers. Before that she had made herself transparent so that I could write . . . Mixing-up of roles. For months long I had been her mother. I felt like I had lost a daughter.

Then again, about his mother's death:

Do not say mourning. It's too psychoanalytic. I'm not in mourning. I'm suffering.

And an even more heartbreaking paragraph:

In the corner of my room where she had been bedridden, where she had died and where I now sleep, on the wall against which her headboard had stood I hung an icon – not out of faith. And I always put some flowers on the table. I do not wish to travel anymore so that I may stay here and prevent the flowers from withering away.

I reread this line: *I do not wish to travel anymore so that I may stay here and prevent the flowers from withering away.* So sad. Unbearable. This love for his mother had to be the deepest love Barthes experienced.

'I know it's a different kind of love. But even if Barthes had loved some men, it would be nothing compared to his love for his mother, right?' When I said this to you, I felt a total revelation about the author.

'Yes. But it's more this: any romantic love would not be able to gain space if the person were totally tied to his maternal love.'

I thought of what you just said. I didn't know about you, but I sensed that neither you nor I were totally tied to our mothers or our fathers. Did that suggest our romantic love would be strong and complete?

Barthesian Love Discourse 3

*– As I understand it, for Barthes, the deepest love was not
sexual. It was beyond sexual.*
– Beyond sexual! That was exactly how I felt.

Then I thought about my relationship with my parents. My
father was perhaps the only man I loved deeply, but I never
expressed this love to him. It was not our culture to express
love in a verbal way. The only physical intimacy between us
that I could remember was when I was a child and we tried to
cross busy roads – he would hold on to one of my arms and I
would cling on to him as cars roared past. Both my father and
I were short-sighted, and we worried about each other whenever we walked in busy streets. Otherwise, our bodies were
apart. Just as our goals in life were apart. Years later, when he
was dying in the hospital, I had held his hand. His skin was
wrinkly and leathery, and felt damp and cold. That was the last
moment our bodies were near to each other.

I was not so close to my mother, even during the final
months before she died. She was not a tiger mother like other
Chinese women who were strict with their children. But she
was unaffectionate. She never enjoyed her life. 'To live is just
to suffer. Nothing good comes out of it.' That was her daily
motto. She believed this for all her life, and she wanted me to
believe it too. Perhaps it was because of the hardship her family had suffered in the past, or because of the total lack of any

education. For her, life was only about dealing with practical matters. Anything non-practical for her amounted to stupidity. And I was very impractical. I wanted to write and make films when I was at school. Later on, when I became an adult, I chose to study something which would contribute nothing to practical day-to-day life. 'Eat to live, or live to eat?' She would scorn me. And it was so clear for her that there was only one answer: 'Live to eat.' That was why, from when I was quite young, I had talked only to my father. But my attachment to him ended when he passed away. And when my mother died, my attachment to China began to die too. I came to Europe. I wanted my adult life to be in Europe. Now as I thought of my love for you, it was like an extension of my love for my father, or a father in a different land, who would teach me how to live, away from familiar landscapes and languages.

'As I understand it, for Barthes, the deepest love was not sexual,' you remarked. 'It was beyond sexual.'

'Ah. Beyond sexual!' I looked at you.

That was exactly how I felt after being with you for almost a year. We went through the first winter together, and we were still very much in love. My love for you was to do with this boat life, this water, this landscape, and where we would finally moor.

THREE

东

EAST

Self-indulgence &
Self-absorption

– Do you like Duras's work?
– Oh, please. She is such a pain. A perfect case of
self-indulgent self-absorption.

When I read Duras's *The Lover*, I could see vividly in my mind's eye the interactions between the young French girl and the Chinese man, their conversations, their ways of making love. I felt keenly the power play between the two. He is rich but he is Chinese. She is poor but she is European. Which character did I immediately identify with? It felt natural to me to identify with the French girl. I would behave exactly like her. But why did I not identify with the Chinese man, since I too am Chinese? For me, being female trumped everything else. I felt *everything* that French girl felt. Absolutely everything. Even though I had first read the book at university in China, and had never travelled abroad at that point. I hadn't felt any cultural barrier between my life and the French girl's life. Strange. But there it was.

The different kinds of sensuality expressed by different authors seemed to be a primal factor in my reading experience. There was always a barrier for me to cross when I read books by male authors. The sole exception was Barthes. Barthes was like a woman who could not stop talking. A good woman brimming with words. I always had problems reading Balzac, Dickens or even Hemingway. Somehow I found their tone pompous, and their unbending masculinity was impossible for me to penetrate. Only when I found paragraphs that carried a sense of the defeated, the ignored and the dying did I feel connected. Only then did I feel at last there was something in their books that I could get closer to. Then I remembered reading an interview with Duras. She was talking about how she felt suffocated by reading classical novels, especially Balzac. She pointed out that Balzac describes *everything* in his books. Absolutely everything. And it's exhausting for readers. In Balzac's novels, *there's no place for the reader*, I remember Duras said.

I felt the same with most of the classical novels taught at school. They were too male, too indigestible and too exhaustive.

'Do you like Duras's work?' I asked you.

'Oh, please,' you said, showing the white of your eyes as they rolled upwards. 'She is such a pain. A perfect case of self-indulgent self-absorption.'

'Fuck you! I am asking you about her work, not her as a person!'

'Is there any difference?' You looked at me, with a mocking smile. 'She is totally narcissistic. A narcissist can't love anyone but herself.'

I was angry. In my eyes, great writers, singers and artists were usually narcissistic, but we loved them nevertheless. That was because they were reflections of ourselves, our lives and our minds. How could you separate *us* from *them*? Or maybe you were scared of emotions, and didn't want to be too close to certain ideas about yourself?

Vaterland / Fatherland

– In this case I prefer the German – Vaterland, *rather than motherland. I rather think China is my fatherland.*

– But in our Vaterland *we still speak* Muttersprache.

During my second summer in Britain, the trip came. And I had to leave you as well as the boat or I would fail my PhD. I told you that I would only be gone for two weeks. You said you would miss me. But you would occupy yourself with work on the boat and on some landscapes. 'I'm very used to being *alone,*' you added, and then in hesitant Chinese: '*yi ge ren*'.

Yes. *Yi ge ren.* Alone.

After handing over a dozen administrative forms, and receiving signed permission from my supervisor, I took some camera equipment with me and left our boating life for China. I was flying to a hot and bustling southern province near Shenzhen. I was not going back to my home town, a home town with two new gravestones and sombre memories. The umbilical cord was finally cut, forever.

'In this case I prefer the German – *Vaterland*, rather than motherland,' I said to you, before I headed off to Heathrow. 'For me, I rather think China is my fatherland.'

'But in our *Vaterland* we still speak *Muttersprache*,' you responded, walking me to the train station.

After a long and agonised flight, my plane landed in Shenzhen. Heat and dampness kissed my face as soon as I got off the plane. Tropical plantations with large leaves and bright red rhododendrons welcomed me by the highways. Here I was, back in my country after a year as a researcher, with foreign eyes and a Western perspective. I liked this feeling, I thought to myself. So I didn't need to bear the heavy weight of this country. I was just passing through, like I was passing through England.

I found it strange – this word *fieldwork* in anthropology study. 'Field' made me think of the yellow soil, paddy fields and deep mountain valleys where I came from. And fieldwork was compulsory for university students and professors during the Cultural Revolution in China. Farmers were our teachers. But these days, there was not much 'field' left to work, especially in the West. As a would-be film anthropologist, I was heading to a modern industrial Chinese 'village'. There, everyone worked and lived in their concrete blocks, their bodies hooked to numerous mobile phones and video games – an electrical field, a technical farm.

When I arrived in the village, I found myself a cheap hotel called South Star. It was located at the junction between the artisan village and the motorway which led to the throbbing heart of Shenzhen. I had been to Shenzhen in the past, but I had never visited this village on the outskirts. I checked in, and entered my room. It was late, but I didn't want to sleep, and could not sleep. Wasting no time, I put down my camera equipment and walked into the village.

It was about ten thirty at night. On the boat in England, I would be in my pyjamas hugging my hot-water bottle on the bed. But here, the day was just cooling down. Colourful neon lights glowed everywhere, especially in front of workshops and food stores. All sorts of advertisements, from karaoke bars to hair salons, from acupuncturists to MBA courses, all shining in the night sky. On the roadside, accompanied by music from the shops as well as their smartphones, people were drinking their noodle soup and talking loudly. Some seemed to be quarrelling over their meal and it looked like a fight was on the way, but very quickly a burst of laughter washed away the argument. Kids ran around in the night alleyways, water guns or battery-operated toys in their hands. So colourful, so full of life. This was something I didn't have in England. The vitality. It was an essential thing I missed when I was away from my native country. What is more important, I asked myself: the vitality of Eastern life, or the order of Western civilisation? Sitting on a bench under the street lights aimlessly like a foreigner, I didn't have the answer.

An Ordinary Tradesman's Job

– It's an ordinary tradesman's job, why do you want to waste time recording this?
– Maybe it's ordinary. But I find it interesting.
– No. It's just placing one bit of paint on another.

The next day, after sleeping in my sweat without turning on the air conditioning, I woke up in a sticky and slimy bed. It was almost forty degrees, and it was not yet noon. The humid subtropical climate affected my body with a very different metabolism. I was longing for an iced Coke, but there was not even a fridge in my hotel room. Only a plastic kettle sat by my bedside, waiting for me to boil some water.

I took a cold shower. I'd almost forgotten the feeling of standing under a cold shower – something I had not done since I left China. Memories of childhood summers returned to me. I saw myself waking up from a siesta and eating a bowl of iced mint jelly, or killing mosquitoes with an electric fan in our backyard, or stealing watermelons from a field with the neighbourhood kids. Back then my father was healthy and happy. I could always turn to him if my mother was hassling me to do something I didn't want to do. All this was gone now. People grew old, became ill and then died. And I had become a grown-up. Now I was a woman who lived in a cold northern country, trying to build my life with a white man, a WASP.

After the shower, I put on a light dress and opened the window. The heat outside seeped in and soon evaporated my melancholy. I went down to the street with my camera equipment. By the road, I ate a bowl of wonton soup with two steamed buns as the dust rolled past. Right next to me, painting workshops and art stores lined up. You could find a copy of any artist you liked displayed in the shop windows: Monet, Van Gogh, Kandinsky, Pollock, Chagall, Renoir, Picasso, Matisse. There were also the classical Chinese ones too, the inky landscape scrolls from Tang Dynasty Wang Wei and Wu Daozi.

I entered one workshop, then another. After chatting with the workers, I checked a few more stores. It seemed to me that this artisan village was based on a traditional working household: the husband would be painting a Monet while his wife prepared a new canvas and the grandparents cooked in the back. At the same time their cousin or uncle would be making a picture frame in the yard, ready for the newly painted Monet. They spoke of simple things, and did not have much education. Almost all of them were migrants from poorer parts of China. They were easy to talk to, and almost oblivious to my camera.

'It's an ordinary tradesman's job, why do you want to waste time recording me?' The worker spoke in front of his painting, yawning, and carried on applying colour to his Monet.

'Maybe it's ordinary. But I find it interesting.'

'No. It's just placing one bit of paint on another.'

He opened his mouth wide, making another loud yawn, and took a break from his *Water Lily Pond*. He drank a mouthful of Coke, reaching out for a spiced chicken foot on a plate next to his paints.

All afternoon and into the evening, I wandered through a maze of workshops, filming the artisans working. It was always the same: their shopfront displayed the paintings they had copied, and the family would live in the back or upstairs. Every house was a self-contained factory, with adults labouring away, and kids studying or playing in the yard. This was not so different from where I came from. In my home town, one street would produce large quantities of shoes or clothes with all family members involved in the labour, while another street would specialise in hardware products or, say, herbal medicine. As we say: *fei shui bu wai liu* – 肥水不外流: don't spill your soup outside the house, and keep the best cuts for the family.

Klimt's Kiss

– Did you paint this Klimt?
– Yes. I was so bored copying that I changed the man into
a pig for fun. Don't take it too seriously!

Then I saw a large reproduction of Modigliani's *Nu Couché*
hanging at the front of a corner shop. The reclining red nude
looked very striking in the shadowy alleyway where peasants
and workers rushed back and forth with their goods bundled
on their motorbikes. A static two-dimensional sprawling body
in the flow of street life. As if under a spell, I walked towards
the painting. It looked almost authentic, and beautiful: the
elongated eyes, the black hair, the breasts and nipples, as well
as the brown pubic hair. It was clear that even a copy of the
original was attractive. I liked the copy, though I remembered
the original in Tate Modern was much darker, not so red. This
Chinese worker loved red too much. Perhaps he thought it
would be more eye-catching? Perhaps Amedeo Modigliani
would not have been too upset if he had discovered his most
famous painting had ended up here, as a reproduction. At
least he might be happy that his nude woman was not cen-
sored here, in a still Communist China.

Behind the red nude, through the lit window, I saw a man
cutting a watermelon for his two small children. An electric
fan spun on the ceiling. Behind him, an unfinished Klimt's
Kiss. But when I looked carefully, I saw it was not exactly

Klimt. The male figure who was kissing the female figure had been given a pig's head. How incredible! Had the painter done this? It reminded me of the Nigerian American portrait painter Kehinde Wiley who had copied Caravaggio. This was like something Wiley might have done. I thought I should just walk in and film this man. With the watermelon and the pig-headed Klimt's *Kiss* it would make a good scene.

'Did you paint this Klimt?' I asked the man, pointing at the pig head.

'Yes. I was so bored copying that I changed the man into a pig for fun. Don't take it too seriously!' The worker-painter laughed, then looked at me with his wrinkled eyes. He put down the dripping watermelon, and lit a cigarette. Then I noticed another painting in the corner: *The Birth of Venus* by Botticelli. The central figure was not Venus but a standing goat! As I stood there in amazement, children ran around me screaming and fighting. Now one of them grabbed a smartphone and began to play a video game.

The worker-painter seemed a little uncomfortable with the attention I was giving to the goat *Venus*. He hurried to put away the Klimt and Botticelli mockeries, and placed the perfectly copied Modigliani piece in front of me.

'Do you like this?'

'Yes.' I nodded. 'How much are you selling this for?'

'This is my display copy so I need to keep it. If you can wait a day or two, I can paint a new one for you for about 250 yuan.'

Did I really want this piece of reproduction? Just for academic interest? I asked myself. Perhaps not. Maybe I should ask him to paint something from Leonardo da Vinci that would be a good present for my professor in London. He had just emailed about my fieldwork. Would Prof Stanley like to have a large *Virgin of the Rocks*, or even *Salvator Mundi* above his office desk? I pondered.

The Virgin of the Rocks

– The rocks are easy to paint, but not the angel or that woman.

– The woman? You mean the Virgin Mary?

I decided not to buy the Modigliani reproduction. Instead, I would film Li Bing painting da Vinci's *The Virgin of the Rocks*. And I would take that to Britain. He asked about *The Virgin of the Rocks*. He had never painted it before and didn't know it. He had done the *Mona Lisa* dozens of times for his customers, though he didn't think it was beautiful as a painting. It usually took him two days for a *Mona Lisa*. 'But after I finish the painting, it will take more days to dry. And my hairdryer is old and noisy.'

I showed Li Bing an iPhone image of *The Virgin of the Rocks*. He then found another picture on his phone. The version he found was the Virgin Mary in a blue robe, not a green one. This was the version hung in the National Gallery in London. He looked at the image for a few seconds, and frowned.

'I will need at least three days to do it.' He shook his head. 'Too many people in it: two women and two babies. Plus those strange rocks! They are like our crazy mountains in Guangxi Province!'

I nodded in agreement. Yes, four figures in one picture. Not like the *Mona Lisa*, which Li Bing would have done in no time.

'The rocks are easy to paint, but not the angel or that woman,' he remarked.

'The woman?' I enquired. 'You mean the Virgin Mary?'

'Oh, is she the Virgin Mary?' Li Bing took a closer look at 'the woman'. 'But she has the exact same face as Mona Lisa! She has got the same hairstyle as Mona Lisa, and the same eyelids! Even the neck is the same: short and thick!' Li Bing cried out.

I glanced at the tiny image on his iPhone. Well, Li Bing was not completely wrong. Virgin Mary or Mona Lisa, she was probably drawn from the same model da Vinci had used. Who knows?

'Anyway, the angel is complicated to paint. Her wings are barely visible, and all that fabric!'

Angels. We had *Feitian* in our mythology – flying ladies in the sky playing musical instruments. *Feitian* would also be complicated to paint, with their floating figures and elaborate robes.

Li Bing promised me he would try to finish it as soon as he could, on the condition that he would need to drink with his friends and play card games every afternoon and evening. I said no problem. I would wait, if it was only three days.

Li Bing gave me a discounted price for this da Vinci piece: 380 yuan. That would be around fifty US dollars. I was happy with the deal as long as he let me film the whole process. Though I did wonder to myself – if he must play card games for half of the day, when would he have time to paint? Only in the early mornings?

Family Economy

— Right, family economy. What about your children? Will they have the same job when they grow up?
— No way! They will have to get an MBA!

It was almost noon when I woke. I had a quick wash and went to the same roadside stall for breakfast. I ate two eggs: hard-boiled in green-tea broth. This was something I had always eaten in China, especially in the mornings. While I ate, stray dogs and hens wandered around me, looking for scraps of food. I threw half an egg to a hen, and watched the chicken eating a chicken egg. Doing so reminded me of the old conundrum. Which came first? The chicken or the egg? I stared at the chicken, momentarily mesmerised, and imagined that in devouring the egg it gave the answer.

It was already afternoon. I decided that I must check how Li Bing was getting on with da Vinci. But when I got to the studio, I saw Li Bing's son playing outside. He was targeting a cola bottle with little stones. I asked where his father was, he informed me that he was still sleeping. I went inside anyway. In front of a large half-white canvas, I found Li Bing's wife leaning forward, working on a painting.

There were four figures sketched onto the canvas. Their composition seemed to be set with pencil marks: the Virgin Mary, the Christ child, the infant John the Baptist and the angel. The rocks were not there yet. Nor any plants. Holding a small brush, the wife was colouring Mary's blue dress. She left her face untouched. I stared at the faceless Mary, a bit perplexed.

The wife, in her mid-forties, seemed to know her job well. From time to time, she picked up her phone, and enlarged the image to check some details. She then applied the paint onto the canvas. When she saw me, she greeted me with a Sichuan accent:

'Here you are! Li Bing drank so much last night, I thought I should speed things up!'

I was curious to see the way she painted.

'Where did you learn to paint?' I asked, and at the same time took some photos with my phone.

'Where? Right here!' She pointed to the floor she stood on. 'The first three years after I married him, I would just stand behind him while he painted, watching how he did it. Then a few years later, I thought: I can do that too. So I started to help. Since then we have four hands to earn a living, not just two!' She laughed. And then added: 'The government encouraged family economy, and we followed!'

'Right, family economy. What about your children? Will they have the same job when they grow up?'

'No way! They will have to get an MBA!' She laughed again, loudly. I could hear the kids in the background playing video games.

I observed the way she painted Mary's robe – the dark and complex folds, the soft drooped edge. Did she think about perspective? Or the direction of light? Then suddenly I noticed that she was using Chinese ink on her colour plate. She ground an inkstick in a mortar, and applied the natural ink onto

Mary's dark dress. I was astonished. The Chinese inkstick was used for traditional ink-wash painting. I didn't expect to see it used for a Western oil painting.

'So you prefer to use stone ink rather than black oil paint?' I enquired.

'Oh, I dislike black oil paint. It's too thick, too dead. Chinese ink is better,' she answered, her eyes not moving away from the canvas.

Too thick, too dead. Chinese ink is better. I brought out my notebook, writing down her words. Then I praised her skills, and began to do some filming. It was not until much later in the afternoon that her husband got up. Heavily hung-over from the night before, his first words shouted out through the turpentine-filled air:

'Wife! Cook some porridge. No alcohol today! Just por-ridge with pickles!'

Halos

– *When are you going to paint the halos?*
– *What halos?*

The next morning, the sky remained grey and dark, and the air was suffocating. A huge storm was building somewhere in the South China Sea. The weather report warned of a typhoon that would arrive in the afternoon. Strong winds swept every movable thing in the streets. The uncollected wooden frames and canvases were scattered about like dried leaves. Workers rushed out from their shops to rescue the tools of their trade. I could see a tall tree swinging violently at the far end of the street like a marionette on a string.

With his wife's help, Li Bing had almost finished the four figures as well as part of the rocky landscape. By evening, he was working on the chubby body of baby Jesus – in fact I doubted if he knew the baby was Jesus. Would it change anything, though, if he learned who was who in this image? I didn't want to interfere. Instead I just observed the way he painted Jesus's arms. The two raised fingers of the left hand, a characteristic Leonardo gesture. Li Bing slowed his pace down, his brush hesitated and made a subtle movement here. The dusky light descended, bringing cool breezes into the stifling studio. Surprisingly, he didn't seem keen to go out tonight.

'I drank too much last night. Puked twice.' He burped.

I could smell garlic on his breath.

'I can finish the background details tonight, then it can dry tomorrow.'

I nodded, and continued to film him working. But when I looked closer at the painting, I saw that neither Mary nor Jesus had a halo around their head. So I reminded Li Bing:

'When are you going to paint the halos?'

'What halos?'

'The circle of golden light around their heads!' I pointed to Mary and Jesus. 'You know, the thing a saint would usually have.'

Staring at his work, Li Bing looked confused. Then he took his phone from the stand, and studied the image carefully.

'Ah, halos!' He was exasperated. 'I didn't see them until now. The picture is so small on my phone!'

He put down his phone and looked again at his work. Hesitantly, he said: 'Do you really think we need to add the halos? I mean, everything is great on this painting, but halos? They make the picture look amateurish. No one has a halo! People would think that was naughty graffiti from my son!'

I didn't object to his view on halos. Without them, I should pay less for the finished product, but I didn't want to say so. He had let me film whatever I wanted – that was more important than adding two halos to the picture. In the middle of our conversation, rain had started spraying through the half-opened windows. A paper napkin blew onto my camera lens. Then all of sudden, a great mass of water came down from the sky. Li Bing and his wife got up and rushed to close all of their windows. His wife hurried out to buy candles.

'There was a power cut twice last month – we'd better prepare!' She ran into the street with the rain now pounding the ground with a wild din.

'You'll probably need to wait two more days for the paint to dry,' Li Bing added. 'With this weather, it will stay wet, unless you buy me a new hairdryer!'

Okay, a new hairdryer. I nodded, without a word.

Memory & Architecture

– Do you think memory constructs architecture, or does
architecture construct memory?
– Both, or maybe neither.

Two days before I left China, I took a bus and travelled around
the outskirts of Shenzhen. Only two hours away, towards
Fujian Province, numerous villages and rice paddies appeared.
The mountains were green and blue and dotted with houses.
Then I saw the ever-familiar water buffaloes, treading ponder-
ously through swampland. By the rice fields there were
sweet-potato farms, their heart-shaped leaves spreading out
furiously and forming entangled vines. This was the landscape
I grew up with. This was the landscape in which I had lived
before my family moved. My father had found a job in the
city, and my mother wanted to leave the farming life. Everyone
was leaving their farming life back then. In my *laojia* – old
home village – we had water buffaloes and I used to ride on
their bare backs when I was a child. But after I finished primary school, our field was obliterated by new roads and we
sold our house and the animals. We moved to the fifteenth
floor of a brand-new tower in an industrial town. Once or
twice we went back to the old village – but it was now a
double-lane expressway dotted with traffic lights. On both
sides of the road, more construction sites. There was no sign

of rice paddies, buffaloes or farmhouses. The landscape I had known from childhood had been erased.

I thought, if you were here with me, I would ask you this:

'Do you think memory constructs architecture, or does architecture construct memory?'

What would you say? You probably would say something like:

'Both, or maybe neither.'

And I imagined my frustration with your answer. Our conversation would probably go on like this:

'What does that mean?'

'It's our memory of the unattained and something greater that leads us to construct architecture. But at the same time, architecture is the house of all our memories.'

Would I be satisfied with your answer? Not sure. Architecture is the house of all our memories? My memories of childhood were to do with farmlands, mountains, and the creeks that seeped into our fields and disappeared underneath our feet. And my memories of the teenage years in the new town we moved to were about how my parents tried to adapt to urban life, an industrialised life, and how my heart longed for something greater, something far away but beautiful, something more imaginative. Was all this part of your grand house of *architecture*?

FOUR

北

NORTH

Rootless Generation

– Rootless generation? I don't feel I am rootless.
– You might not feel that way. But I do. And this kind of
life has made me feel even more rootless.

Two weeks had passed in southern China under the sun, in a whirlpool of human interactions. I hadn't missed you at all. Nor had I missed London. I thought of you all the time, but I didn't feel that I needed to return to you, or return to the boating life. In this semi-tropical Chinese province, there wasn't time to be lonely. Lonely was not even a common word here. I had almost forgotten about our *Misty*, until the moment my feet touched the path of the Regent's Canal.

I dragged my suitcase along the narrow asphalt. It made a sad sound, and echoed above the dark water. Suddenly, China became the past again, even though the heat was still stored in my hair, in between my toes, and under my skin. Soon the memory of the tropical heat was replaced by the English wind.

Autumn had turned gloomy. It was cold on the boat. But you didn't seem to mind. The first night after I got back, you burned coal in our little metal fireplace. I noticed that you had made more repairs and sealed the cracks around the windows and doors. You'd bought a new engine too.

'Do you feel better now? Less cold?' you enquired.

'Well, yes. But I feel very jet-lagged.'

But was I really jet-lagged, or was I caught in the stark contrast between the tropical village rhythm and this confined boating life in northern Europe? Even with your father-like care, somehow I felt the life we shared now was simply a camping life, a childish life, a life without roots.

'I was reading the paper on the plane, and they used an expression *rootless generation* to describe the current twenty- and thirty-something people who grow up in urban spaces.' I paused. 'And I felt we are that generation.'

'I don't feel I'm rootless. And I'm passing my mid-thirties.'

'You might not feel that way. But I do.' I gazed at the water, imagining we were surrounded by floating lotuses and dancing dragonflies. Suddenly a gust of wind came and the lotuses dissolved. Only the rippling dark water remained. 'And this kind of life has made me feel even more rootless.'

I thought about those workers in south China, who spend their days painting copies. And the sweaty afternoons I'd spent in their studios with their children and grandparents, filming and eating watermelons. Did they feel the same rootlessness? Despite the fact that their city life was cut off from their past, these artisans still lived among their families with a village life-style. Were they happier, even though they were poorer?

Over the next few nights, I could not stand sleeping in the boat unless it was heated. You went to buy charcoal. I looked for abandoned newspapers. I found plenty of discarded copies of the *Daily Mail* and the *Sun* outside Tube stations. We lit the paper in our stove. It was a bit warmer, but we inhaled fumes every day. Coughing in the smoke, I joked bitterly:

'My potential cancer cells are being rapidly activated with this lifestyle, but it's romantic. So I can die early without complaining too much.'

You didn't seem to want to comment on that.

'You know, every year thousands of Chinese women die of lung cancer, even though they have never smoked in their life. But they spend their days in kitchens breathing in gas and fumes until cancer takes them. That's what happened to one of my aunts.'

You remained silent.

The fumes grew heavy. I could not open my eyes. Leaving the cabin, I stood on the deck to get some fresh air. It was dark and cold outside. I looked at the houses by the canal – those warmly lit windows inhabited by *normal* people, normal families with proper gas pipes and heating and loos. We had all that before. Why did we abandon it?

Future Continuous Tense

– I shall be *going soon.*
– Oh, why? I thought you didn't have to he at work until
tomorrow.
– But I shall be *preparing on site.*

We had been on the move for two days, because we had to get to a new mooring. Now we were miles away from Victoria Park where we used to moor. The new area was not as pretty, and our only view was of a massive rusty gasometer. But there was space for *Misty*. At least there was no double mooring. I felt that I had just come back from China, and now I had to get used to a new place again, and to find out about the nearest shops and toilet facilities. Was I a gypsy's wife?

And once we were settled, after a few nights, you got up and said:

'I *shall be* going soon.'

'Oh, why? I thought you didn't have to be at work until tomorrow.'

'But I *shall be* preparing on site.' You added, 'I need to know the place as much as I can. Besides, the company still haven't sent me the contract.'

The contract. Yes, I knew. Your contract would bring money, but I didn't remember the last time you had a contract. That was another issue. But right now, there was this issue – your verbs and especially your linking verbs were strange. Perhaps I should learn a man's character by paying attention to the way he uses verbs. I found it difficult to understand the way you used the *future continuous tense*. I hadn't learned to speak like that. I was still a foreigner, a linguistic outsider.

Really, how should I understand this 'I shall be working . . .'? Did you feel you were wasting time at home with me, and wished to be somewhere else? Or did you feel guilty about not working as much as you should? Either way, you didn't want to be on the boat with me. What if I just went out, and stayed in the British Library all day? Would you feel more at ease alone? I didn't want to ask any of this. I just watched you gathering your paper and your laptop. You kissed me, unloaded your bike from the roof, and said you would be back around five that evening.

The Garden of Cosmic Speculation

– I can say our kitchen sink is more like a black hole than this garden.
– Well, I say you still don't understand about landscape.

It seemed while I was away, you'd begun to receive more work commissions. You had a garden design project in a national park in Wales, then you got the go-ahead to restore a dilapidated mansion house in Sussex. You must have been so relieved that you could get out from our enclosed cage and be somewhere else. One morning, you told me:

'I have to be away for quite a few days, maybe even two weeks. To work.'

'Where?'

'Scotland – a forest park near Ae.'

'Ai?'

'It's spelled A-e.'

'Is it a town?'

'It's a village, near Dumfries. Have you heard of Dumfries?'

'Dumb Fleece?' I shook my head. All those names sounded strange and ancient. Were they Celtic words? 'What will you do there, in Dumb Fleece? Design a fountain? Repair a church and relocate their gravestones?'

'Oh, please. Give me a break!'

I didn't want to be too invasive, so I stopped asking. But then you explained with some patience: 'The area has a large conifer forest, and now they want to build a lake with a pavilion by the edge of the forest.'

'Build a lake?'

'Yes, why not?'

'Hmm . . . I'd love to come with you.' I suddenly felt curious.

'Are you sure?' You stared at me. 'It will be wet and cold there.'

'Well, I don't want to be alone for so long,' I confessed. 'I can work on my thesis wherever you are.'

You nodded.

'If you come, I'll take you to the Garden of Cosmic Speculation. It's close by. You'll like it.'

'The Garden of Cosmic Speculation?' I repeated in awe. This sounded ten times more interesting than living on the boat.

But I didn't expect the journey to take so long. The public transport was bad in this country. It wasn't that far, but it felt like the amount of hours we spent on the journey would have gotten me to China or America. Not to mention the cost of multiple train fares controlled by different railway companies. Before even getting close to Scotland, we had already changed trains three times due to delays and cancellations. By the evening we were still in miserable England, not getting any closer to our destination. We waited and waited on some desolate platform in one of those sad little towns. Finally, the next morning, we arrived at 'Dumb Fleece' about twenty hours after we'd set off.

Two days later, after your meetings with the locals to discuss your plans, we hired a car and drove towards the place you'd promised: the Garden of Cosmic Speculation. On the bumpy road, looking at the pine forest passing outside, I imagined a mysterious park with simulated Milky Ways and magical vibrations in the woods. But when we got there, I realised that words were just words, the fantasy was nothing to do with the reality. It was not an unearthly place we were throwing ourselves into. First, we had to line up to buy tickets. Really? Tickets to *the landscape*? While I waited at the entrance, you found out you'd got a parking fine and you had to move the car.

When we finally got into the 'Cosmos', I wasn't at all impressed. There wasn't much forest, just ordinary hills and ordinary greenness.

'This is a bit like what I do with outdoor spaces,' you explained. 'But of course I have never been given such a space to design. Nor would I ever own such a place.'

'You never know, maybe one day.'

'Maybe.' You sighed.

I found the leaflet in my pocket.

'It says this garden design is inspired by science and mathematics.' I read it out loud: '*The landscaping is based on themes such as black holes and fractals.* Fractals? Maybe. But black holes? Seriously? If you say this garden has a relation to the idea of black holes, then everything has! My hair, your ears, your ass, anything!' I grumbled, walking on to a 'designed' hill with neatly shaved grass. 'I say our kitchen sink is more like a black hole than this garden.'

'Well, I say you still don't understand about landscape.'

You frowned and shook your head. Perhaps you thought of me as a primitive or a philistine when it came to modern aesthetics – or was it postmodern? You walked ahead of me as if to avoid having to listen to my undeveloped peasant views. When we stopped by a small artificial lake, you contemplated the still water and said:

'I like this place.' Then you gazed beyond the water. 'I also love many other landscapes this architect, Charles Jencks, designed. He managed to combine the natural features with man-made curves in an organic way.'

In an organic way. Hmm. I opened my eyes wider, trying to decipher the secret of this man-made land. But the strong Scottish sunlight and blasting winds forced me to close my eyes.

Making Meanings in Space

— I'd rather have mountains with forests, animals and farmhouses in which people really live, than trees encased in iron and designer hills.

— But a great architect is not concerned with vernacular or domestic function. He is interested in space, and making meanings in space.

Standing by the edge of the 'black hole' in the Garden of Cosmic Speculation, my dead mother's old motto entered my ears: 'Live to eat, or eat to live?!' I didn't know why the words had come to me at this moment. Was it because this place reminded me of the cemetery where my parents were buried? Or was it because these surroundings were utterly 'unliveable' according to my parents' vision of life? For them, all actions and efforts were about surviving, not about fun or play.

I took a more careful look at the 'nature' around me: the bent 'trees' made from aluminium, the metal spirals wrapping around branches, the repetitive patterns on the lawns. There were not many plants or trees. Nature had to sacrifice itself for the architect's grand design. Did architects strive for this sort of landscape? I found myself speaking with my mother's logic, and asked:

'Is landscape architectural? Or is architecture a form of landscape?'

You turned round, leaving the lake behind you.

'What do you mean?'

'I mean, isn't all this some postmodern superfluous industrial excess? I'd rather have the natural design of a real landscape, not designed by an expert. I'd rather have mountains with forests, animals and farmhouses in which people really live, than trees encased in iron and designer hills.'

'But a great architect is not concerned with vernacular or domestic function. He is interested in space, and making meanings in space,' you argued.

I stared at the shaved hills and tamed woods in the chilly wind. There was little life here. My primitive thoughts begged for a satisfactory answer from you.

'What is the meaning of this?'

'Well, what's the meaning of anything?' You raised your voice, getting annoyed now. 'You could say love, life or cosmos, they are the same – meaningful or meaningless. It all depends on how you project your views onto things.'

'But don't you think our world is overdesigned and overmanipulated?'

No reply.

'What is the *cosmic speculation* going on here anyway?'

'It is a speculation about the nature of the cosmos. So, questions such as: does the cosmos last forever? Is it infinite space? Is the universe ever-expanding? And so on.' You paused, then said: 'But we can never answer the cosmic questions.'

'Why?'

'Because the universe goes on forever, and we humans are temporary, accidental beings. How could we know its infinity? That's why we want to play with landscape, so as to express these intellectual ideas. That way, we hope to find some connection with the unknown world.'

I thought about this for a while, as we walked along the little path on the hills, in the treeless forest. My views were slowly changing. Perhaps you were right, I could understand a bit more now. Still, it felt strange. Humans are the strangest things. It is absurd that we have deciphered so many meanings about love and about life. And yet the cosmos is indifferent and bears no explanation of our emotion at all, just like the Chinese idiom – 无我, *wu-wo*, no self, no subject. We are not *the subject*. It is not about us humans. Let alone designing nature. So why do we look to the stars all the time in search of meaning and answers? Is it because this is the only way to keep us moving forward? But moving forward to what? Into a vast black hole?

Glazing

– There seems to be no glazing on this copy.

– You are right, they don't know about glazing. But they also don't know which one is Jesus and which is John. For them, knowing the difference is like knowing who is the General Secretary of State and who is the chairman of the Central Party Committee. It's all the same anyway.

At first I didn't show my supervisor the footage from the Chinese village. Instead, I showed him the present I had bought for him from my artisan worker Li Bing.

Behind his desk, Grant opened the rolled-up canvas. His eyes glistened when glimpses of dark green rocks appeared. A lingering smell of oil paint instantly changed the stifling musty air in his office.

'What is this? Leonardo's *The Virgin of the Rocks*?' Grant erupted with fruity sarcasm. 'Did you steal it from the Louvre?'

I tried not to laugh, and said with seriousness: 'No, this version is from the National Gallery! The police are now after me!'

'Ha, I should be careful then!' Grant put on his reading glasses, his index finger touching the Virgin's robes. 'Actually it's not bad. Oh, it's still sticky.'

I watched him, holding my breath. Would he notice that neither Mary nor Jesus had a halo? But Grant seemed to be carried away by other details. His eyeline moved from John the Baptist to Jesus, and then he fixed his eyes on the black rocky mountains in the background.

'Well, these mountains are almost like those depicted in Chinese paintings! Some people could probably tell the copy was done by a Chinese artisan.'

He didn't spot the missing halos. Maybe Li Bing was right. Halos would make the painting look amateurish, or rather, more fake.

It seemed that Grant liked the painting. But then a look of hesitation appeared on his face. Now he sat back, further away from the painting. Should a PhD supervisor take a present from his PhD candidate? Especially when the present is da Vinci's *The Virgin of the Rocks* – even though it was a hand copy of the original?

'Did you buy it?' Grant asked.

'Of course. Three hundred yuan – that's like thirty-five pounds!' I quickly decided to reduce the actual cost by ten pounds. It would make my supervisor feel better.

'Seriously?' He shook his head in disbelief.

Our meeting was an appointment to discuss my thesis, and some major revisions that he had suggested. But we didn't have time to talk about that at all. Instead we discussed da Vinci's painting at length – I mean, the worker-artisan's copy of the da Vinci. Grant asked me what the village was like, how many could paint without any training, and how did the workers paint shadows when they had only iPhone images as a reference.

'I think you are doing a very valuable piece of ethnography!' My supervisor praised me. 'It's also timely that you discuss the significance of artisans and reproduction in the current commercial world. I hope you made plenty of notes.'

'Yes. I wrote a whole new chapter, and got about sixty hours of footage.'

Grant smiled at me, and then continued to study the faces of the Madonna and Child – their faces had a strange quality under the fluorescent light in the office. They looked slightly Chinese.

'I'm really interested in knowing more about their actual painting process – maybe you can show me some footage next time. There seems to be no glazing on this copy. Do they care about this sort of texture?'

'You are right, they don't know about glazing. But they also don't know which one is Jesus and which is John. For them, knowing the difference is like knowing who is the General Secretary of State and who is the chairman of the Central Party Committee. It's all the same anyway.'

Grant nodded, though seemed unconvinced, even bewildered. He now raised his eyes, looking at the white wall above his desk, which was pinned with various university schedules and conference leaflets.

'Do you think it's a good place for her?'

'Sure, you can pray to her before your lectures,' I quipped.

Grant laughed.

This was indeed a better present than the melted chocolate, I thought to myself.

Britain is Sinking

– Look at the title: 'Britain is Sinking'.
– Oh, how surprising!

I stared at the water. The algae had been growing so much that it now covered this part of the canal completely. Weeds were everywhere as far as the eye could see. There were no ducks, since the weeds had changed the movement of the water. It was totally static. There were dead fish. Occasionally I could see their white bellies turned upwards, floating, clearly no longer alive. The algae had invaded their space and had sucked the life out of the water.

Then I thought of the Grand Canal in Beijing. It was built thousands of years ago and rebuilt by later dynasties, to provide a transportation link between northern and southern China. When I first went to Beijing to study, I went to visit the Grand Canal with my father. Only two days before, we had arrived in the capital and registered at the university. My father had to return to our home town the next day. So we came to see the famous canal together. It was September and still very warm in Beijing. I remember the sun was piercing and the air was dry, even though only two months later it would snow heavily. A desert climate, I later learned. There were old willow trees standing beside the Grand Canal, their trunks bending and their long branches coming down to the water with elongated leaves swinging back and forth. The water was yellow – it was the colour of the sandy and muddy Yellow River nearby. At that time, the water was still flowing, but there were no boats at all. We were told that it was forbidden to use boats on the canal. We didn't know why. We would have enjoyed boating on the ancient Grand Canal. There were many things forbidden in Beijing, as I would increasingly discover as each day passed at the university. For example, no protests, no marches, even CNN news was forbidden. But that day, I was new to the city, just as I still felt new to London now. That day, my father brought a bag of food with him, and we sat by the bank, eating our lunch under the September sun. I remember my father said:

'I am glad that you are studying in this city where the Grand Canal of China began. We are proud of you.'

In the lunch box my father had brought, there were buns and cut sugar cane. My father had bad teeth. All his real teeth were gone. He had replaced them with a set of porcelain teeth years before. He gave the sugar cane to me, and ate his bun. The next day, he set out for the railway station. He had to sit on a hard seat for twenty hours to get back to our home town. Perhaps his cancer was already growing in his lungs at that time. We had no idea. Just as I didn't know that I would land in Brexit Britain rather than a more prosperous Western country.

Now in London, as the cold season approached, the greenness of the algae had become duller. One afternoon, you emerged from inside the boat carrying a newspaper, pointing at a headline.

'Look at this,' you said. '"Britain is Sinking".'

'Oh, how surprising!'

I took a look, and saw the subheading: 'Sinking, Both Geologically and Economically – Britain on the Way Down'.

On the second page, I read an article about immigration. It said that since the Referendum, more EU citizens had left the UK than had arrived. Well, I didn't know how this would impact my stay here, and our boat life. I had heard mooring in Germany was free. Could you move this boat across the Channel to get to the other side? Was our *Misty* strong enough? Or was it just a whimsical, cheaply constructed lower-class craft?

Machine for Living

- *I'm not that interested in whether buildings should have ornaments or plain straight lines. I prefer Le Corbusier's vision: a house is a* machine for living.
- *A machine for living? Isn't that a very male way to think of a house – as a machine? For me, to be alive is not to be a machine.*

I woke up at the third geng. Listening to you sleeping soundly, I got up and moved over to the table. I switched on the small table lamp. In front of me was a stack of designs you had drawn. I had never tried to look at your landscape designs before. Perhaps I feared I would find them too abstract, too mathematical. And, I felt, there was something totally disconnected between designs and practical environments. I felt I could not trust what was drawn on paper. But now, in the quiet hours, I had some time to kill. Actually they were not real drawings. They were computer-generated drawings, with perfect curves and lines for some buildings that looked like exercises in brutalism. I thought, I hate buildings with perfect curves and lines. It was obvious to me that such designs were not for humans, but for robots. Architects had forgotten the obvious.

I was impatient for you to wake up, so I could point out the errors of your ways. Finally, you stirred. And I had a cup of coffee ready for you. I put the cup under your nose, and remarked:

'I am not a fan of brutalism. I don't understand why people think brutalist buildings are fashionable, or cool. Why can't we admit they are just ugly, cold and barren?'

'Bullshit. Some are amazing.' You groaned and sipped your coffee. 'What about the Barbican Centre? You like that.'

'But that kind of building is not for living. For shows and exhibitions, yes. So much concrete, so few windows. If you live in a place where you are cut off from light and nature, and regular communication with other humans, it is easy to become lonely and depressed. Don't you think? Look at these houses around us!'

You raised your eyebrows, and began to tidy up the drawings on the table. I could feel that you were in one of your morning moods and didn't want to launch into a debate.

'Tourists always want to go to historic cities with beautiful old buildings and natural landscapes, but never new towns with grey soulless slabs. Tell me, how did contemporary architecture wind up like this?'

You wanted to start your work, and you didn't want to pursue this conversation. 'The short answer may be: this type of architecture is produced by contemporary global capitalism. It demands more generic, standard and non-ethnic products.'

But I was not convinced. 'This cannot fully explain why architects no longer want to design ornaments and to deliver more humanistic styles.'

You finished your coffee and now found some eggs for breakfast. At the same time you reluctantly gave me a brief history lesson in modern architecture:

'There was an Austrian-Czech architect called Adolf Loos. He lived a hundred years ago. He wrote a famous essay in 1908 called "Ornament and Crime".'

'"Ornament and Crime"?'

'Yes, this architect declared that a lack of ornamentation was a sign of spiritual strength. He introduced plain, stripped-down buildings. He thought ornament on buildings was like a corruption, a feudalistic gesture.'

I was taken aback. I felt irritated by such a statement. It sounded overly political, like some kind of fascist propaganda slogan. Was there any connection between ornament and lack of spiritual strength? The Forbidden City was full of orna-ments. No one would dare to say that there was no spiritual strength there. And his name was Adolf Loos? Very strange name, I thought.

'Isn't Adolf a very unpopular name? And, Loos? Both bring very unhealthy associations.'

You chuckled. 'Just a bloody ordinary Austrian German name at that time. Adolf Hitler was only a school student then. No one thought "Adolf" was evil!'

'Whatever. So what else did this Adolf Loos say in his propaganda essay?'

'Lots! He explored the idea that the progress of culture is associated with the deletion of ornament from everyday objects, and that it was therefore a crime to force craftsmen and builders to waste their time on ornamentation.'

'He sounds like a cold-hearted industrialist. A house should be personal and full of character! Don't we have enough of these boring modern buildings? Even if his theory was right, what's the difference between forcing craftsmen to make ornaments and forcing them to build those grey sad Bauhauses?'

You thought for a bit, and nodded, only slightly, with your forehead creasing. 'Well, I'm not that interested in whether buildings should have ornaments or plain straight lines. I prefer Le Corbusier's vision: a house is *a machine for living*.

'A machine for living?' I considered these words, then asked: 'Isn't that a very male way to think of a house – as a machine? For me, to be alive is not to be a machine.'

You now stared at me as if I were a rather dull student who had made another banal remark in class. At that moment, your expression reminded me of my professor, who was an expert at these withering looks.

'I don't think you understand Le Corbusier yet. What he meant was a house should have organic functionality.'

Ha! *Organic functionality*, another empty term from another 'expert'. It sounded like a glorified compost heap. If a home had organic functionality, where would I put my imagination and my fantasy in this machine? I was sure that you had a different idea of a machine. It was not part of my vocabulary, for describing ways of living.

Later on, when I had some free time, I looked up this Adolf Loos. The article I found said this supposedly great modern architect was convicted as a paedophile in 1928 for abusing girls from poor families from the ages of eight to ten. Oh well, so much for an influential theorist in the development of modernism. His 'Ornament and Crime' would have been a better essay if it had been linked to his own crimes, his crimes of pleasure built upon young girls' misery. I guessed you knew about this part of his life too, but you could separate the man from the theory, whereas I could not.

Fernweh / Distance Pain / Wanderlust

– I can't find a similar word in English. It's a German word – Fernweh.
– What does it mean?
– It can be translated as distance pain, an ache or a lust for a place where you want to belong. Do you have this Fernweh, *sometimes?*

As the days got shorter and colder, we stayed inside more and more. Sometimes you went to work, and I was left alone to write in the boat. But I would spend time staring at algae on the water. Something was missing in our life, but I was not sure what it was. One evening, you brought back a Chinese takeaway to cheer me up. It tasted awful. Nevertheless we ate it, and talked.

'I can't find a similar word in English. It's a German word – *Fernweh*.' You frowned.

'What does it mean?'

'It can be translated as distance pain, an ache or a lust for a place where you want to belong. Do you have this *Fernweh*, sometimes?'

I nodded. *Fernweh*, an unfamiliar word, but a familiar concept to me.

'It's funny we Germans speak of *Weh*, pain, while the English for *Fernweh* is *wanderlust* or *travellust*. I feel more pain than lust.'

'Hmm, I feel more lust than pain.'

'So where is the place that you think about?'

'Often I dream of living in a tropical land with lush vegetation growing all around me, and I can see the sea or mountains in front of my house. But I tell myself not to indulge in this fantasy too much. It will only make me sad.'

'Have you been anywhere like that, or even close to your fantasy?'

I thought for a while. Searching for a place outside of China. Sadly, I had visited very few places in the world. Come to think of it, it was a particular location in Australia.

'Maybe Australia, the country you grew up in.'

'You mentioned that before. But still, half of Australia is desert. It's not that great!'

'Yes, but it was my first trip abroad after college. For some reason the travel agency took us to Cairns, near Port Douglas.'

'Cairns?' You chuckled. 'No one goes there apart from Chinese tourists!'

Ignoring your laugh, I continued: 'When we stepped out of the plane, I felt that my skin was melting in the hot wind. We were dispatched to a hostel near the beach. There were mango trees everywhere. That was the first time I had ever seen real mango trees in my life. Those mangos were golden-yellow and ripe with a strong sweet smell. The air was heavy with their odour. Next evening, I sat on a porch eating my supper, and saw those big bats flying in between the mango trees . . .'

I could visualise the scene right now: the waves in the distance and the wind. I remembered the wind was so special there, mixed with the scent of ripe fruit and the salty sea.

'That first night I sat on the porch in our hostel, watching the moon going towards the west. I didn't feel lonely at all. I had this strange being-at-home feeling. What's that word again? *Fernweh*. It almost made me sad. I felt this was my fantasy land. Every hour I spent there was magical, every minute reminded me of a home I had never had.'

You listened to me attentively. Your lips revealing a smile. Perhaps my love for the tropics of north Queensland reminded you of your childhood, and made you too feel a sense of *Fernweh*?

'So why didn't you try to stay there? Or go back there?'

'Well, I thought it wasn't real. I was too young, had no purpose in life yet. I stayed in north Queensland for a few more days, before boredom gripped me again.'

I stared at the canal. This was the English water, cold, grey and full of deadly discharge. It was incomparable with the water in Queensland. No mango trees. No giant bats. No tropical fruit smell. Just a few ducks floating by, with their feet trapped in plastic shopping bags.

'So what about you?' I asked. 'Where is your *Fernweh*?'

'I sometimes miss the east coast of Australia, even though I left there long ago,' you murmured, as if just speaking the words *east coast of Australia* already transported you to that continent. 'When I first came to Germany, I remember I hated the dull winters which seemed to go on forever, and how we were stuck indoors. And even the snow seemed to be grey. I missed the ocean, the bush, and going surfing during the school holidays.'

The evening wind came, sending shivers onto the water, as well as into our bodies. The coriander I grew on the deck was also shivering. The coriander – I noticed – had grown a lot. Their leaves spread out among weeds. And I heard your voice again:

'My family used to have a beach house near Melbourne. My dad painted the walls a different colour every two years. I remember he was always fixing something at that house – engines, motorbikes, any rusty machines he had collected . . . And my mother would just wear a swimsuit all day long, even when she was cooking.' You paused. Then you sighed: 'But then, we left the place and the ocean altogether, for Europe.'

'Maybe we should go back to Australia. It's too cold to be on the boat at this time of the year,' I said, half serious.

'Well, my aunt still lives there with her husband. She'd love us to visit.'

We looked at each other, both smiling. Then you started to laugh. You seldom laughed. In my memory you only laughed in a sarcastic way. But this time your laugh was not ironic or sarcastic. It was genuine and innocent.

FIVE

下

DOWN

Surf

 – *I miss this light, and these waves. I used to be a surfer,*
  but now I don't remember the last time I was in the
  water on a board.
 – *But you told me your knees hurt when you surf.*

Queensland in November. It was summertime in this part of
the world. The days were very long here. Time seemed to be
stretched. The train from Brisbane airport to Cleveland took
centuries to arrive. The sunrays painted leaves inky green,
black-and-white magpies stood on treetops mysteriously. The
train dragged itself along slowly. So few people were on it. A
sense of self-abandonment was diluted in the hot air. The train
seemed to know there was no reason to hurry, as if there was
not much going on at the end of the line.

 A burnt forest came into view as the train moved along.
The earth was black, like in a horror movie. You stared at the
passing scene, pondering something beyond words. For you,
it must have been a sentimental but alienating trip: you left
this land so long ago. Everything must be familiar but also
foreign. Sitting opposite us were a dark girl and a white boy,
kissing. I wondered if she was Aboriginal. She was young, perhaps sixteen or seventeen? After a while, the lovers looked a
bit bored, and opened a packet of crisps. A void in their eyes.

 In the distance, the sea appeared. The real blue foamy sea,
without much algae, without the ducklings we had lived with

side by side. This was a sea with strong oceanic swells, and occasional dangerous aquatic life.

'I miss this light,' you said, 'and these waves. I used to be a surfer, but now I don't remember the last time I was in the water on a board.'

'But you told me your knees hurt when you surf.'

'That's bullshit. The reason I don't do it is that there are no decent waves in Britain. You wouldn't call them waves. The breaks are too small. The water in Europe is sad. There's no real blue in it.'

The water in Europe is sad. I thought of what you said. If so, the water in China was even sadder. On our coast there were so many rusted hulks, abandoned factories, beaches crowded with people stripping them of seaweed and shellfish. The sea was grey and churned up like a dirty and crinkled canvas. I wondered what you would say if I took you to China.

Working-class Paradise

– Have you heard Australia is called a working-class
paradise?
– A working-class paradise?
– I didn't understand it when we lived here. But now, I
agree with the cliché, if I had to compare it with the
working class in Britain or in America.

We arrived at Coochiemudlo Island. It was near Moreton Bay by
the Port of Brisbane, in the South Pacific. You told me
Coochiemudlo is an Aboriginal name. It means red rocks. 'It's
very small, only five square kilometres,' you warned me. I checked
it on the map before we left the mainland. It was a tiny dot in the
Coral Sea. We might as well go to Fiji or Tonga, I half joked.

The island is close to the bay, but it felt like an island adrift
from the world. There were A-shaped timber houses situated
along the hills, and some were buried in the woods. The landscape was beautiful, the air fresh. We came here because this is
where your aunt and her husband now lived. Your aunt's
house (you called it a *bungalow*) sat right next to the water's
edge, with palm trees in the back and bottlebrush bushes
growing in the front. When we got closer, I saw a barbecue
and beach chairs on the lawn. I imagined spending my days
lying on one of those beach chairs, bathing in the sun with the
sound of the waves. Would I feel this was something I finally
wanted to achieve in life?

'Have you heard Australia is called a working-class paradise?'

'A working-class paradise?'

'Yes. I didn't understand it when we lived here. But now, I agree with the cliché, if I had to compare it with the working class in Britain or in America.'

I saw what you meant. The barbecue, the warm wind, the blue sky and the white beach. All this promised a pleasant life. The dry bottlebrush flowers and spiky thistles in front of your aunt's house signified the truth – not elegant but pleasant.

'This landscape somehow guarantees a decent life – not highbrow, not so sophisticated, but agreeable.'

'Guarantee?' A strange word to use, like something from a TV ad.

'Yes. As long as it is not too crowded, it brings about a certain promise, even though it can be just as problematic as anywhere.'

As long as it is not too crowded. When I thought of what you said, an image of the Swiss landscape entered my mind. Or a postcard with Stockholm Palace above blue water. I didn't think what you said was true, though. India and China are very crowded, and don't these countries bring promise and happiness to their people?

Your aunt, who was your mother's older sister, had retired from city life with her husband. She opened the house for us, a few old fat cats following behind. Your uncle had a loud and jolly voice. He was suntanned, wrinkly but healthy-looking. I imagined he didn't have arthritis or rheumatism like us folk from wet lands.

Inside, the house had a stale and musty smell. The stink of cat urine. The carpets were as old as your uncle, with dark brown stains here and there. There were quite a few rooms in this house, but each was cramped with old books and damp boxes and cracked furniture. They showed us our room – another dark room with a very old sunken mattress. I thought the dark and staleness inside made up for what was outside – the sunny, dry wildness. God knew about irony. God might be from Australia too.

Nostalgic about England

– Are you nostalgic about England yet?
Not yet. I am still looking for my Fernweh.

The rainstorm arrived in the afternoon, after a very hot noon. The raindrops formed a wet curtain, sweeping across the island. The old gum trees, the mangroves, the yachts by the beach, as well as everything else on the island, were under a sudden attack of green-blue torrential rain. From the house, we could see some children still swimming in the bay, with their colourful swimsuits. They were called back by their parents. Within minutes, the beach was empty.

The storm didn't move away. It stayed for hours on end, wrapped around the island like a great amorphous animal, squatting over us. I was not unfamiliar with rainstorms. I had known such heavy rains from my childhood. But not at this time of year – in the middle of November! This was the southern hemisphere – we were upside down. In the night, raindrops leaked through the windows. They came down where our bed was. I sat up, waking you and switching on the light. I thought, no wonder the house smells so musty and damp. It leaks. And then I heard another strong blast of wind. Everything was rustling madly. The gum trees in front of the window swung back and forth and it looked like the trunk was going to snap. Your uncle got up. He switched on the light and went to the front door to check something.

In the midst of the wind and rain, we couldn't hear the seagulls. There was no human voice on Coochiemudlo, not even a dog barking. Only the waves, the rain and the wind.

The next day, the wind had ceased and the sky was once more dry and blue. There they were, your uncle and aunt, moving their old skeletons in the house and outside in the garden. I watched you making a list of things you wanted to buy for them: batteries, fruit, vegetables and meat, toilet paper, and so on and so forth. To go shopping on the mainland, we had to wait for the ferry which came only once every two hours. I walked to the beach, and stared at the sea with some stale bread in my hand. Yes, the ocean out there is boundless, but humans don't really belong to the ocean. Humans belong to the land. Land only.

'Last night the storm caused a power cut, and destroyed the converter, so now we can't use computers or any of the main lights,' your uncle said. 'I hope you'll get used to the loud generator in the back, I have to switch it on now.' His face broke into crackling laughter.

The generator was switched on. No more sounds of waves or wind. Only the drone of a whirring machine and the stink of oil.

'We've been travelling for a while. Sydney and Melbourne were nice, but now we're marooned on this island. Are you nostalgic about England yet?' you asked.

'Not yet. I am still looking for my *Fernweh*,' I said.

'In this case, I would say you're looking for your *Heimweh*, your *Sehnsucht*,' you corrected me. 'Your longings, or your desire, if you like.'

Aussie Salute

– *Have you heard of the great Aussie Salute?*
– *What is that?*
– *It's this: you wave your hands to scare away the flies!*

All the romantic stories are flawed. Or if there was ever a romantic one, it would come to an end. Since we arrived on this island a few days ago, you had told me some affectionate and beautiful stories about your aunt and your uncle, and how they had travelled the world on their sailing boat. Now, in this musty crumbling house, one of your cousins came to visit. Robert, but your uncle called him Robbo. 'How you, mate?' – that was Robbo's greeting to me. I nodded, but didn't feel I was his mate yet. Robbo liked barbies. He threw a chunk of frozen kangaroo meat on the fire, while you prepared some salad. Bottles of Victoria Bitter (a big local brand) were bought from the shop, and you even managed to repair the old dusty stereo to play an LP version of Beethoven's Ninth Symphony. When the meat was cooked, a seemingly very local conversation began. 'A cold one!' 'Deffo! I'm going for a ciggy!' 'It's for your brekky tomorrow!'

I tried a piece of kangaroo meat. It tasted like the buffalo meat I ate back in China.

Then you asked me: 'Have you heard of the great Aussie Salute?'

'What is that?'

'It's this: you wave your hands to scare away the flies!' You waved your hand, chasing away the cloud of flies over the meat.

I too did some Aussie saluting, and at the same time, heard more jolly good old Aussie slang. I thought, this is a light-hearted family, relaxed and easy-going. But in no time the family was arguing about money. The old couple said they had no money and Robbo was angry. The atmosphere grew heavy. You listened to their conversation patiently, without commenting. I stood up, throwing some meaty bones to the cats. I thought, luckily they are not your parents. And you are not the person asking for money. But perhaps this was just a rehearsal for me?

Leaving the fly-infested table, with kangaroo meat in my stomach, I climbed onto the slightly damp bed to read my book. *Zorba the Greek*. That was another sunny land I would like to be in. Maybe one should always dream of sunny lands but never be in them.

A Wide-screen TV

– *The sea in front of them might as well be the sea on a wide-screen TV.*

– *Well, not quite. The beach is sacred for Australians. It is only a TV screen for you because you have little connection with this sea. But it's different for them.*

We were on a train, then on a bus, and then in a car, passing through Queensland and heading towards New South Wales. Vast land. Vast emptiness with bright sunshine on deep green trees. So strange, the name of every town here came from England, even the street names: Queen Street, Adelaide Street and Richmond Road. Colonial identity was fully present. Even though this identity was artificial – this sunny dry land had little to do with the rainy cold country called Great Britain. Did they not want to escape from the old Empire? Instead, they tried to bring it with them.

The Gold Coast is a newly developed tourist town, implanted in what was once a desert by the beach. Fast food, cheap-looking holiday apartments, endless freeways, amusement parks, even the ocean looked plastic here. A great celebration of banality. A complete exploitation of wild nature.

'Don't the developers consult landscape architects before they put up those tacky amusements parks right next to the sea?' I asked, as if this awful industrialised seascape was your fault. 'Is it not the job of a landscape architect?'

You shrugged and simply said:

'The local government and the developers would always choose the cheapest and most profitable proposal amongst all.'

Standing by the ocean, I told myself to face the sea only, and never turn around to the sight of McDonald's and the ugly motels. Perhaps people here were used to the surroundings. They were lying in the sand, bathing in bikinis, drinking from cans.

'The sea in front of them might as well be the sea on a wide-screen TV.'

'Well, not quite,' you disagreed. 'The beach is sacred for Australians. It is only a TV screen for you because you have little connection with this sea. But it's different for them.' Then you added: 'They do all sorts of things by the sea: camping, barbecues, swimming, surfing, making bonfires, singing.'

Singing? I looked at you. Were you being serious? You mean someone like Nick Cave? But didn't he move to England a long time ago?

We left the Gold Coast with a hollow feeling in our hearts, and headed to the next destination: Tweed Heads, and then to Kingscliff, then Hastings Point and Suffolk Park. McDonald's, KFC and petrol stations had taken over the horizon. Strange, where were my mango trees and giant bats? Where were the magic and the mysterious nights from years ago when I was travelling alone and looking for *home*?

The romantic island no longer exists.

I remember the feeling of looking at ancient Chinese ink paintings when I was still a schoolgirl, and how beautiful the landscape depicted in those images seemed to be. And how I would spend time looking for hills and rocks and bridges which resembled what I had seen in those paintings by the old masters. But the painted landscapes were never to be found, or never came alive in front of my eyes. Where were they? Either they had never existed and were just inventions in the minds of the artists, or they had been destroyed by those who came later, people who were in love with new technologies and man-made nature.

无我 – *Wu-wo*

– What do you mean by wu-wo*?*

– It's like no self. No I. Non-existence. My body is here, but I don't feel I am here, right now. I don't feel my existence in this environment.

Through the foliage of the pine woods, we were looking towards Mount Wellington. A deep sense of *wu-wo* rose.

'What do you mean by *wu-wo*?' you asked.

'It's like no self. No I. Non-existence,' I answered. 'My body is here, but I don't feel I am here, right now. I don't feel my existence in this environment.'

How could I explain this feeling to you? I was not a subject in these surroundings, even though I was able to sense the feelings of no self. If you asked an old Chinese sage about *wu-wo*, he would probably say it's the state of human and nature being at one. They have merged with each other. It means the positive disappearance of the individual self, the sage might have added. But here, facing the direction of the South Pole, I was not sure that this *wu-wo* was a positive feeling. I missed the human world and the warmth and chaos it had generated. If we died here, no one would ever notice our death.

But this feeling of non-existence was soon swept away by a nasty reality. We woke up one hot morning and discovered we had been attacked by bedbugs in the night. The bedbugs in the hostel had almost eaten me to a real *wu-wo*, a non-existence. My neck was red and swollen with small bubbles, my arms and legs too. I thought only old rotten cities like London or Paris or New York hosted these parasites, but here, under the purest sky and cleanest air, the army of bedbugs was the strongest and fiercest.

We drove away from the city, and came to the area where the South Pacific Ocean and untouched beach were the only visual elements. We rented a beach house. We made love. Food. We needed food. In a nearby town, we bought a giant calamari, almost half a metre long. We brought back the huge creature, and cooked it on a small stove with salt only. We chewed the half-roasted calamari. Both of us didn't speak much. We seemed to have lost language in this place, or lost any desire to use it. Or perhaps in this place language had lost its meaning. And I was not sure if I liked or disliked this feeling.

In the evening, someone was playing a ukulele on the beach. The tune was slightly broken, but with a bit of the Japanese style. The sound dissolved in the ethereal air above the waves. The moon was full. The tide was rising, as if it were going to reach the silver sphere. Then the waves reached us, sweeping the mossy rocks under our wooden house. I thought of England, and then China. So far away.

'Do you miss Europe now?' I asked.

'Yes, I think so,' you answered. 'I miss the culture.'

I nodded in agreement.

It was time to leave. I missed the big grey dirty urban city with human interactions, and those dimly lit bars and cafes where I could eat through my money as well as chew on my occasionally heavy thoughts.

SIX

上

UP

Lifeless

– Why do you think home is lifeless?

– I don't think home is lifeless. This boat's our home. But I think an enclosed space with a conventional set-up is lifeless!

We finally landed. My body still held the heat from the southern hemisphere but English snow fell as soon as we stepped out of the plane. Yes, snow, come! I yelled in my heart, looking up at the sky and feeling energised by the cold. But the white flakes didn't come down as much as I hoped. We had a lengthy wait at passport control, as the immigration officer asked endless questions about my UK visa and scrutinised each page of my passport. When we left the airport, the snow drifted away. There was only sad wet sludge on the ground.

Returning to England was a peculiar feeling. Sitting on the Heathrow Express and gazing out, the small squat Victorian houses behind winter hedges seemed to mirror my grey mood. I wondered how strongly an urban landscape could shape people's spirit. Was this the land I had missed, and wanted to return to when I was in Australia? I thought about the criticisms I made when I was on the Gold Coast in Queensland. Maybe I was spoiled by the sun. Light is the primary thing in life, I now realised. And culture might be secondary.

The cross-continental travel was only a distraction from the everyday problems we had in London. The boating lifestyle made many simple things impossible. With your eco-friendly solar energy system, which I hated, I had to fight to get my camera charged along with my editing machines. There was not enough power. Then there were bigger issues. Would we live here forever? Would we raise children on this boat? How would we take them to school if we had to move our boat to get legal moorings every few weeks? How would we cope with drunken neighbours on the next boat and always having to pick up broken bottles the next morning?

We had discussed these problems. And I wanted to find a flat again.

'Even swallows choose not to nest on the roof of a boat. You know that?' I put two bowls of instant noodle soup on the table and sat down. 'Yes, even birds prefer to make a home on stable structures. They make their homes in solid trees or under bridges. But never on a moving object! I am the same. I want to have a solid home in a solid place.'

You shrugged. You were not interested in the idea of abandoning boat life.

'We will have the same problems with a flat. Bad neighbours, less outdoor life, and more bills to pay.'

'But at least I wouldn't need to worry about the battery all day long, or whether I can poo or not when there's no water in the tank.'

You didn't respond. But a bit later you remarked:

'Living in a flat in this country makes me feel claustrophobic.'

'Claustrophobic? I didn't know you felt that bad!'

I pondered this word *claustrophobic*. I hadn't heard this word before I left China. We didn't have the same word or even concept. I didn't know how to spell it. In my ears it sounded like *closed-for-peek*. But now if I checked the Chinese dictionary, the word would be listed there and translated into *you bi zheng* – 'the disease of fearing enclosed spaces'.

'But we can find a nice home with a balcony or a garden. Or at least a place with huge windows.' I tried to persuade you.

'You just want to have a comfortable domestic space.'

'What's wrong with that?'

'Well, there's no challenge in it! There's no life in that kind of space!'

'Why is there no life? Why do you think home is lifeless?'

'I don't think home is lifeless. This boat's our home. But I think an enclosed space with a conventional set-up is lifeless!'

I stopped and thought about what you said. Then I suggested:

'But we need a stable address, don't you think? This is not sustainable.'

'This is very sustainable. It's your mind that's not sustainable.' You went out onto the deck, leaving the door open and letting the cold wind into the boat.

The next few days we continued with the same arguments. I began staying away from the boat. I would stay in a breakfast cafe for hours just to avoid the dreary cooking on the boat with limited gas supplies. Or I stayed inside the British Library. I only came back in the evenings. I would arrive with some cheap takeaway, often soggy rice soaked in oily sauce. And you would just eat a plate of salad, barely washed, straight out of a Tesco shopping bag.

Monolingual

– I'm monolingual.

– You can't say you're monolingual.

– But I really feel I am. Whether I speak English or Chinese.

New Year's Eve played out against a background of lilting music with some of your colleagues in their house all the way down in south London. I didn't know them well, nor did I drink any alcohol. I felt desolate and just wanted to go home. With the distant sound of fireworks exploding under the English sky, 2018 arrived. 'Happy New Year!' Everyone hugged each other with zeal and conviction in their voice. I felt I was unable to participate in this ritual. Why *Happy New Year*? A new year was nothing to do with happiness or unhappiness. The time wheel turned forward persistently, without caring about us at all. I had only one more year left on my visa. And after the Dog Year of 2018, where would I go?

While I was waiting for you on a sofa in the corner, you were in your drinking and talking mood. You were deep in conversation with some German friends, moving quickly between English and German. I could not follow at all. I heard each word you spoke but I didn't understand any of it.

I was surrounded by white people. White Europeans, talking and laughing. I thought, even though I speak English, and I can read and write in English, still, I feel monolingual. Really, I had only one language. And even worse, I could not possess this language. It alienated me and it was never mine. I didn't know why I felt this way. Whatever I spoke, whether it was my borrowed English language or my native Chinese Mandarin, I didn't feel I had that language in me. That language spoke for me, instead of my speaking it. That language had existed before me and would continue after me. And I just wore it like clothes. Then it would abandon me when I die.

'I'm monolingual.'

'You can't say you're monolingual.'

'But I really feel I am. Whether I speak English or Chinese.'

We had left the New Year's Eve party. You were yawning and I was waking up in the cold wind. I was not sure that you really understood what I was trying to say but you didn't ask more about it. This made me wonder, do you sometimes feel you are monolingual, even though you were brought up bilingual? You didn't seem to want to follow me in this train of thought, but I really wanted you to know that I felt impoverished and was suffering quietly every day somehow, in my verbal existence, thus my very own existence.

Privatisation of Nature

– *But at the same time, I dislike the practical challenges of designing a house like Fallingwater. It is the privatisation of nature.*
– *Privatisation of nature?*

From the end of January, I spent almost every day in the library. I was getting close to finishing a draft of my thesis. Every evening when I got back home, you would be in front of your computer. A half-eaten banana or apple core next to you. You looked melancholy. Your mood was like the lead-coloured winter sky outside, heavy and despondent.

'What's wrong?' I asked.

You didn't respond. You inserted a piece of bread into the toaster, and just stared, waiting for a burnt slice to jump from its metal mouth.

'Is it to do with your work?'

You breathed out heavily and shook your head. Then you said: 'There was a big project that I was pitching for. But I didn't get it. They've gone for a boring cheap design instead.'

'Why?'

'Why? My design got rejected either by the environmentalists or by the councils. My proposals are always too expensive. So now, with my fancy ideas and high costs, all I can design is my own toilet!'

Your toast jumped out and I watched you buttering it, feeling your quiet bitterness.

'If you could choose, what would be your favourite project?' I asked, trying to lift your mood. 'Would it be something like . . . hmmm . . . Frank Lloyd Wright's Fallingwater, or Chamberlin's Barbican Centre?'

This time, you didn't think my question was silly. You answered without hesitation: 'Fallingwater, for sure.'

Fallingwater is a private house sitting on top of a waterfall in rural Pennsylvania in America. It was featured in a documentary film we watched about Wright. A unique design. This comes across, even in the pictures we saw in the film. But what was it like to live inside the house? I wondered. The ceiling of the house looked very low, and you could not see the waterfall at all from inside, as the house was perched on top of the fall. Would it be lonely to live in such a concrete space, artificially imposed onto nature?

'I think it's inspiring. But at the same time, I dislike the practical challenges of designing a house like Fallingwater.' You munched on your toast, looking thoughtful. 'It is the privatisation of nature.'

'Privatisation of nature?'

'Yes. Rich people getting to own nature, by doing things like building big houses in places of beauty, which really should belong to everyone. And that means no one else can enjoy the waterfall, climb on it or be with it. Imagine a rich person building his villa in the middle of Lake Geneva or Wansee. This sort of endeavour turns nature into a vanity project.'

A vanity project. I remember I read somewhere about Fallingwater, that they had built a driveway to the back of the house, so the owner could drive all the way up to access the home. What a contradictory idea of living in nature. One might as well live in a video simulation with a remote control in your hand.

'Apparently, the owner was unhappy that Wright had designed the house to sit on top of the waterfall. He had wanted it to be on the riverbank facing the falls.'

'Ah, that's the opposite of what a Japanese architect would do!' I had read that Frank Lloyd Wright had been inspired by Japanese architecture. 'Putting the house on top of a waterfall was a *sacro-legion*!'

'What? You mean *sacrilege*, I think.'

'Whatever!'

'Yes, I agree in a way,' you said, and sighed. 'Nowadays, you could never get approval to design a house like that. There're endless rules. An architect can't play too much with ideas any more. We are just better-than-average builders or estate agents, who know the numbers and costs. That's all.'

Again, you looked frustrated. Your mood reminded me of a book I had read – *The Fountainhead* by Ayn Rand. The novel's protagonist, Howard Roark, is an architect who designs modernist buildings and refuses to compromise with the traditional establishment. The critics claim the book is about individualism versus collectivism. But I wondered if the book is actually about man versus nature.

I was going to ask you about the novel and whether you had read it, but you had disappeared into the toilet with a tape measure. You wanted to put in floating shelves and a minibar in the toilet as part of your grand design, on a miniature scale. Oh, how the mighty have fallen.

Historical Records

– *We Chinese have very vague historical records of
everything, especially after the Cultural Revolution. We
burnt everything original.*
– *Unlike us Germans. We record everything, especially the
terrible things.*

Every time I caught a cold or flu I would lament the boat life.
Especially when my joints ached from the damp English
weather. Also, I would moan that I could not cook a slow
hearty soup on the boat to cure my cough.

Very often I would sit on the windy deck to rinse salad
leaves. Pouring the dirty water into the canal, my joints ach-
ing. When I came in to warm up one evening I said with sarcasm, a style of humour I had learned from you: 'I can't wait
to grow older so that my decrepit body can plop into this
beautiful canal and sink to the bottom.'

'Oh, it's all part of the natural process. Soon London will
sink beneath the mud and a new ice age will come.'

As if this useless conversation was not bad enough, I would
then react angrily:

'But it is not that easy to die! We don't just die. We get ill
first and then we suffer for a long time before we eventually
expire. I don't worry about death. But I dread disease and
the long process of ageing and suffering. No wonder some
advanced countries have legalised euthanasia. If only we

knew how much suffering we have to endure before we actually die!'

Your mouth twitched. I could see you were trying not to laugh.

This was getting silly. But I would not stop. I could not resist foolishly reciting a poem from the Tang Dynasty poet Li Bai.

'You remember this Chinese expression *fu sheng*? I explained it to you once – it's in Li Bai's poem?'

'*Fu sheng*?'

'Yes. *Floating life*. In the old days, if a poetic Chinese man felt sorrowful about life, he would speak about his existence as a "floating life" – *fu sheng*.'

'So what did he say about *fu sheng*? Remind me again.'

'One of his poems is called "At a Spring Night on a Banquet with My Cousins in the Peach Garden".'

'Prepositions!' You corrected me: 'You mean "On a Spring Night at a Banquet with My Cousins in the Peach Garden".'

'I hate prepositions.'

'Okay, calm down. But what does the poem say?'

I grabbed a pen, and wrote down the verses, remembered by rote from my childhood:

夫天地者，萬物之逆旅也。
光陰者，百代之過客也。
而浮生若夢，為歡幾何.

'Jesus, that looks so lovely. What does it mean?'

You were impressed each time I wrote Chinese characters, as if you could never get your head around how I managed to remember putting these strokes together in such elaborate patterns. But then equally I could never quite understand how you could remember to put *der*, *die* or *das* in front of each noun.

I looked at the verse for a moment, and roughly translated it.

Heaven and earth are eternal;
Generations pass, mere shadows and light.
Ah, this floating life, just a dream.
Happiness, a deceiving mirage!

You listened, with a smile. Then you repeated:

'This floating life, just a dream . . .' You picked up some salad with your fingers and started to eat. 'And how did he die? All geniuses have unusual deaths, as far as I know.'

'We don't really know how Li Bai died. We Chinese have very vague historical records of everything, especially after the Cultural Revolution. We burnt everything original.'

'Unlike us Germans. We record everything, especially the terrible things.'

'The most well-known version is that Li Bai drowned after falling from his boat when he tried to embrace the reflection of the moon.'

The reflection of the moon. You walked to the front deck, your eyes fixed onto the water. You looked a bit sad, and I knew why. Two days ago, I had found a studio flat in the area at a good price. There was even a small balcony. We could move in any time. But you didn't want to leave this boating life. We could not afford both places. We had to make a choice.

I followed your line of sight, gazing into the night sky. It was a cloudy London night. There was no moon, no reflection. There was only the sound of sirens from the streets cutting through the air and making tiny waves on the canal's stagnant skin.

Art is Gone

– So art is gone, home is not working, what's left for me to hang on to?
– Well, neither art nor home could save you anyway.

When we were in Australia, we had promised ourselves that once we returned to London we would visit the National Gallery. It was probably a conversation we had on the Gold Coast, with the holiday resorts around us. And now, back in London, we had not bothered to visit any museums or galleries. Finally, I erupted:

'Let's go this afternoon.'

'Well, it's a bit late. It's nearly three.' You glanced at your computer. 'Let's do it tomorrow.'

'No. Either now or never. I know what we are like!'

So we dragged ourselves to the Underground and squeezed into a loud train, heading towards Trafalgar Square.

Once we were inside the National Gallery, I wanted to go straight to where da Vinci's works were hung. But you said we should have a look at some of Van Eyck's paintings first. You really loved Van Eyck, especially the one with the couple holding hands – *The Arnolfini Portrait*. So I stood behind you, watching you looking at the painting. Such an awkward gesture, I thought, between the man and the woman. Did that body language explain something of the psychology of northern Europeans? I wondered to myself, looking at your body language. We were very different, you and I, for sure. For example, our chins. Your chin always tended to hold inwards, towards your chest. While mine, outwards, towards others. And then our hands. Your hands were often in your pockets, and mine were always exposed, even in the winter.

When we finally got to the da Vincis, we couldn't find *The Virgin of the Rocks*. I moved about, from one room to another. I really wanted to see the original. Yes, the original! This was a desire that had been growing since I had filmed Li Bing painting Mary and Jesus in that Chinese village. His Mary and Jesus were without halos. At least, I thought, I should check out the *real* halos here. But after looking in every possible room, the piece was nowhere to be found.

Feeling drowsy in the warm museum, I walked to a guard and asked:

'Excuse me, where is *The Virgin of the Rocks*?'

The guard was a middle-aged man in a black suit. He stared at me serenely, and answered with some precision in his tone: 'It is *not on display* at the moment.'

'Not on display?' I repeated, almost offended. 'But why?'

The man in the suit shrugged his shoulders. 'Well, sometimes the paintings are on tour, or being reinstalled. I can't tell you the exact reason.'

You stood beside me, looking just as disappointed as me. What was the point of coming all the way here, changing trains three times, only to see *Not on Display*? I would have brought Li Bing's copy and hung it here!

'So, art is gone, home is not working, what is there left for me to hang on to?' I grumbled under my breath, walking out of the room and feeling weary.

'Well, neither art nor home could save you anyway,' you responded in your usual sardonic way. 'That version was only a reproduction anyway – the National Gallery pretended it was the original.'

'No, there were always two versions! Both are original. One has been displayed here, and the other is in the Louvre!'

'You're right. Both are original.'

On our way out, we stopped in the shop. I found a postcard of *The Virgin of the Rocks*. There they were, two halos, like gymnastic rings, hovering above mother and child.

Quickening

– It is moving!
– It is quickening.

With coal and logs burning in our multi-fuel stove, we stayed on the boat and tried to keep warm. We watched a BBC programme reporting on Brexit and the government's negotiation with the EU. They discussed the possibility of a new referendum and a new prime minister. You were agitated, but you could not stop yourself listening with fascination to any news connected with this act of self-destruction.

I told you I must be pregnant, after missing my last period. You didn't say much, but you looked concerned. I went to the chemist alone, and bought a pregnancy test. Once I was back home, I did the test right away. Positive. Now both you and I felt strangely nervous.

We went to see the local GP – the test result was the same. When we came out, the world suddenly felt different in front of our eyes. The weather warning on your phone read: a new storm is arriving in Britain. In a few days the country would be covered in showers and snow in the north. You put away the phone, and took my hand. We stood on the pavement, gazing at the streets like an old couple, frail and confused. The sky was dark and gusts of wind already descended. The leafless trees somehow looked shorter and thinner than they usually were. The pavement was full of problematic details we hadn't paid any attention to before. Why was the manhole not covered? When did they move the bus stop a few yards away? I noticed children passing by with their mothers or nannies, snot hanging down from their nostrils. Did they know the storm was coming? Everything felt new and abnormal, and everything demanded that I look at it again carefully.

We rushed back to *Misty* before the storm began to swallow the streets. Closing the door behind us, I wondered whether I would get used to this peculiar state of being – carrying a fertilised egg and walking around as it grew limbs and body parts?

You were beside me, and you were involved. But you weren't freaking out as much as me. We began to pay attention to what I was supposed to eat. In the supermarket, we looked for organic products. Was the GM soy milk safe for pregnant women? What about farmed salmon? Too much antibiotic in them? I took vitamins every day. I ate almonds and apples every morning. I made my bras loose, so they wouldn't hurt my swelling breasts. By the end of the fourth month, when I first felt the foetus moving, I was overwhelmed.

'It is moving!'

'It is *quickening*,' you corrected me.

'Quickening.' I repeated this enigmatic word. 'Yes, I really feel the movement of it – the foetus, whatever it's called.'

Who would have the right words to describe the feeling of this little thing *quickening* in my womb? No, it was nothing like a butterfly. Or a small bird flapping its tiny wings. These metaphors were too light and pretty for this sensation. It was a finger tapping inside my lower abdomen, then my uterus tightening slightly because a small bubble was swimming inside. It was indescribable.

CD Player

– *Where does this CD player come from?*
– *From a friend. A goodbye present.*

When I thought of my first pregnancy and the abortion, I saw a teenage girl walking around her southern home town in her blue school uniform. And I saw her carrying a silver-coloured Discman – a CD player – in her pocket. The Discman was very much connected to that event, and I often wondered whether without that little machine I would still have got pregnant.

It was my final year of high school. I was half-heartedly in love with a boy in my class. In my year, everyone was burying their heads in their books in order to pass the university entrance exam. But I was not studying, at least not as hard as the others. My marks were never good and I was convinced that I would not pass the exam. This boy was in the same situation. He told me he would not go to university. Every evening, after supper, the school would remain open till eight thirty for self-directed study. Instead of staying in the classroom, reviewing equations, I would hang out with the boy in the playground. He had a Discman, charged with three batteries, a fancy thing to own at that time in a small town like ours. And he would lend it to me sometimes, with whatever CD was inside. One evening, we wandered into a little forest at the back of our school. In the pitch-black, we sat on the grass. We hugged and kissed. He then played his CD, with one earbud in my ear and the other in his. This time, he had a new album. It was Sinéad O'Connor. And the song we were listening to together was 'Nothing Compares 2 U'. I remember that song very well. Not because I loved the song, but it was very intriguing and exciting for a schoolgirl like me to hear a high-pitched Western woman singing about something I didn't really understand. Before the song was even finished, we were having sex. It was not my first time. But it was the first for him. He came quickly. At that moment I wasn't worried. I thought a woman couldn't get pregnant that easily. It was a chance, or a lottery – according to the older women I overheard. The next day we resumed our revision, half stressed and half bored.

A month passed, and I realised I had missed my period. I started to feel anguished, especially when my mother was around. Even though she knew little about what was going on in my life, I feared she would sense the distress in my silence. I waited for another ten days. Still nothing. I was still seeing the boy, but somehow we were no longer physically so close. He had been under pressure from his parents and had to dedicate all his time to the final exam. He offered me his Discman and said he would focus better without it. I took it and didn't tell him that I might be pregnant. It would be worse for him, I thought, if he knew. I didn't use the Discman very often. I was not in the mood. My body felt alien to me. I felt sick, often when confronted with a meal. Thankfully, I ate lunch and sometimes dinner at school, so my mother didn't notice my nausea. Two more weeks passed, and I gathered some information on what I could and should do. One morning I left school, telling the teacher I was ill. I planned to go to a clinic in a neighbouring town. The surgery would take no more than half an hour – I had read that somewhere. But the bus trip took me an hour and a half. Shortly after I got on the bus, I began to vomit. There were many peasants on the bus, with their baskets of vegetables and caged chickens. Stretching my head out of the window, I puked miserably after each stomach cramp. Despite my physical agony, I worried that if I could not complete my mission today, or if I returned home too late, then the whole world would discover my secret. And if my mother found out, that would be the end of my life.

As I was throwing up, the passengers next to me glanced at me with sympathy. But the driver couldn't have cared less. His foot stepped on the gas pedal and we drove jerkily along the bumpy country road. At that time we had only a state bus service and the driver had to arrive at each stop on time. Finally I got off the bus and found the clinic. I registered myself, and waited in anguish to be called. The nurse came and tested my urine. I was informed that I was definitely pregnant. We were under the One Child Policy then. Abortion was the most common daily practice in any hospital. The doctors and nurses were very efficient at this particular task. I don't remember how long I waited. I sat on a chair in a very shabby hall, with constant stomach cramps and a bitter metallic taste in my mouth, worrying about what would be in store for me next. Finally I was called into the operating theatre. Two women in white uniforms received me with few words. Since I was not a minor, they didn't question me. One of them simply enquired: 'Did your family come with you?' I nodded, lying: 'Yes, they are waiting out-side.' I thought if I told them I had come alone, it might look suspicious. They didn't ask anything more, and just treated me as an object. I imagined they must go through this so many times each day, and they had to finish each procedure quickly so as to get on with the next. I was told to remove my pants and lie down on the operating table. I didn't know what to expect or what kind of instrument they would use. Without warning, a cold metallic object entered my vagina. I was petrified by a sucking mechanical sensation in my abdomen.

An hour later, I was back on the same bus home. I felt sick and weak but, strangely, I didn't vomit on the way back. It was inexplicable, since I had always suffered from carsickness. It was June, and the sky was still very clear and bright. I prayed that the bus wouldn't arrive too late. That evening, when I finally opened the door, my mother was in the kitchen. She was cooking. As usual, she didn't even raise her head to look at me. She simply told me to peel the yams. I walked to the dining table. There, a small basket of yams was waiting for me. I sat down and started to peel them, in silence.

Two months later, I received a letter informing me of the university entrance results. To my surprise, I had been accepted by a university in Beijing. The next day, when my father gave me his old suitcase, the first thing I packed was the Discman.

'Where does this CD player come from?' my father asked, looking at my silver music box.

'From a friend. A goodbye present,' I answered. Then I filled the suitcase with the best clothes and books I owned.

A few weeks later, my father accompanied me on the journey to Beijing. My mother stayed behind. On the train to the northern capital, I thought of my secret abortion, and I said to myself: never ever get pregnant again.

SEVEN

左

LEFT

Marriage of Convenience

– *If we get married, then people will think I just want the* marriage in convenience.
– *It's not* marriage in convenience. *It's called a* marriage of convenience.

The weather was still cold and grey, but we began to go out more. You wore exactly the same padded jacket you'd been in since the autumn, but I wrapped myself up from head to toe. On our way to the Saturday market, we passed a jewellery shop. Normally I wouldn't stop in front of a jewellery shop. Somehow I had never been interested in rings or diamonds. But today I stopped in front of the window, as I saw a ring in the shape of a small leaf. I stared at it, impressed by the design.

You stood behind me, watching me looking at the ring. Then you said:

'I don't understand people's fascination with diamonds. If you think about its material properties, it's just a form of coal.'

This was a very typical comment from you, a non-sentimental man.

'No, I'm not looking at diamonds,' I explained. 'I'm looking at that leaf-shaped ring.'

I walked in, and then realised it was an expensive shop for wedding accessories. Half-heartedly, you followed me in. On the glass shelves, there were pairs of wedding rings for sale.

The salesman looked at us, and smiled.

'Can I help you?'

We shook our heads awkwardly. I was embarrassed. We left the shop as quickly as we could. Once we were back on the street, you asked in a careful tone:

'Did you like that ring?'

'Yes. It looked nice,' I confessed. 'But I don't wear rings.'

You thought for a moment, then said: 'It's actually not as expensive as I thought. Should I buy it for you?'

'No, it's a waste of money.'

This was strange, I thought. I knew you weren't interested in this kind of stuff. What were you up to?

'What about if I buy you a wedding ring?' You looked at me.

'What?'

'Yes, why not?'

'You serious?'

'Yes.'

'But I'm not sure I want to get married,' I said hesitantly. Though I had to admit to myself that I was happy you had proposed.

With a pause, you said: 'But it'll be good for our child, don't you think?'

I nodded. Yes, the baby.

'How about this?' I made a quick calculation. 'Don't buy that expensive ring. Instead, we rent out or sell the boat and then we get married and go on a honeymoon.'

You pondered on what I had said, then nodded.

'I don't want to give up *Misty* . . . but I guess I'll be getting you and the baby in exchange. That's fair.'

The jewellery shop was now at least two miles away, and we had left the market with our hands full of vegetables and fruit. You hugged me by my waist while we walked to the canal. The whole conversation had weighed down heavily on our stroll. When we got to our boat, my mood was lighter and I felt happy. Perhaps *happy* was not a right word. But my future now seemed much clearer. My visa, my legal stay in Britain, all this could be solved very quickly.

'You know, if we get married, people will think I just want the *marriage in convenience*.'

'It's not *marriage in convenience*. It's called a *marriage of convenience*.' You corrected me, quite humourlessly.

'Okay, marriage of convenience. Marriage of helping or cheating for legal status.'

'Well. It *is* a marriage of convenience and that's perfect. I think we should only get married if it helps each other, and if it does, then it's a perfect marriage.'

I was unclear if you were being serious or not.

Then you added: 'Love doesn't need a marriage certificate. We only need that for practical matters.'

'Okay, let's do it – but only on the condition that we won't tell your family now, until we have agreed together on a good time to tell them.' I felt nervous as I hadn't met them yet, and it all seemed quite quick.

You shrugged. 'That's fine with me. My parents are not stuck in the mud.'

Stuck in the mud? I wondered.

Later on that night, we warmed each other under the damp duvet. The boat swung a little in the wind, and I quietly hoped you would not be too sad to lose the boat. Perhaps it was time for you to build a real home for us. A real home. A house with solid walls and proper roofs.

Rights to Marry

– So our marriage plans are kaput.

*– I can't believe it. What about the immigrants and
refugees who come to this country? Without birth
certificates they are not allowed to marry?*

A carp wants to jump over the dragon's gate, but it is still a
carp. There seemed no easy way for me to turn myself into a
dragon. We thought getting married would make my staying
in Britain easier, but it led to a more complicated matter. To
register our marriage, I needed some legal documents. But I
didn't have a birth certificate. Without a birth certificate I
could not register for marriage in Britain.

'Maybe we could go to Germany to register the marriage?'

'Germany?' You stared at me. 'You really don't know how
complicated the Germans can be. The authorities would need
an *Ehefähigkeitszeugnis* before anything else. Jesus Christ!'

'What is that?'

'An *Ehefähigkeitszeugnis* certificate states that there are no
legal hindrances to your marriage in Germany, which means
both people have to prove they are single before the registration. And that is a pain in the bureaucratic ass.'

I sighed.

'But how come you don't have a birth certificate?' you
asked. 'Surely it must be somewhere in a dusty drawer or on a
shelf in your home town.'

'I never had one. We only had a *hukou* registration, which is the household record from the government.'

'So our marriage plans are kaput.'

'I can't believe it. What about the immigrants and refugees who come to this country? Without birth certificates they are not allowed to marry?'

'Well, they probably need refugee documents to prove they don't have a birth certificate. How would you prove that you can't provide a birth certificate? It's all bullshit!'

I thought for a moment, and shook my head.

'Tell me more about this *hukou* registration,' you asked, furrowing your brows.

'Yes, the household registration, but I don't know where it is. If my parents were alive they could help. Anyway, even if it still exists it would have expired long ago. We were supposed to renew our records every few years . . .'

'Why are things so complicated with you? Are the Chinese always so vague?'

I thought about what I could do. Maybe I had to go back to China again, all the way to my home town, to find an authority who could get me a certificate. But the thought of going back to a place that no longer bore the same name and was no longer located in the same administrative area, it was not even physically there any more, killed my desire to return.

Finally, after a few days of telephone conversations with my aunt in China, she agreed to help me obtain a birth certificate. She would need to do some bribing, in order to speed things up.

'As soon as we get the marriage certificate, we'll go on a honeymoon. Don't forget!' I added: 'And the boat will be on sale, as we agreed.'

'You don't need to remind me.' You glanced at me with a sigh. Then you asked: 'Where do you want to go for the honeymoon?'

'Rome!'

I smiled and embraced you.

Power is Beautiful

*— Obviously power is beautiful. Women in particular
know that.*

*— Yes, women are attracted to power, but they don't think
it's beautiful. It's men's illusion to think power is
beautiful.*

There was a moment of happiness after the brief ceremony at
our local town hall, but our honeymoon began with a quarrel.
I wanted to have a short stop in Pisa before Rome, because I
had heard that Chinese immigrants had taken over the town.
But for you Pisa was only a badly constructed tower surrounded by easyJet tourists. And you preferred Florence to
Rome. I said I could not stand the museums and stiffness of
Florence. So we had to choose a compromise to settle the
argument. We went to Lucca.

Lucca is a walled medieval town. We moved about its narrow streets and ate bruschetta followed by endless gelatos. We
visited a hanging garden on the roof of the Torre Guinigi.
The tower is said to be seven hundred years old and remains
intact. In my eyes, a tall tower is a bleak image, a statement of
unfriendliness and exclusion. We had to walk up a narrow
winding staircase forever, but it only led to a solitary sky hole.

'People were mad in the old days,' I said. 'To build such a
tall tower just to demonstrate their power and to compete
with other aristocrats in the area.'

'It wasn't just about power.' You touched the rough wall on the staircase, and examined your dusty fingers. 'The ancient Romans first discovered how to make cement and bricks. That's why the medievals could build really high buildings.'

'So, technology first, beauty second!'

'It's also bloody beautiful.'

'Oh, you mean power is beautiful!'

'Obviously power is beautiful. Women in particular know that.' You said this without irony.

'Yes, women are attracted to power, but they don't think it's beautiful. It's men's illusion to think power is beautiful.'

'Oh, you're just playing with words again.' You left me and strode up the stairs.

I followed you, unwillingly, irritated by your impatience.

We stood at the top of the tower. The wind and height made me dizzy. Vertigo must be to do with unworldly feelings in human bodies. It is not natural for us to stand next to chasms. I wondered how and why other people didn't feel queasy at all on a tower like this. Or was it because of my pregnancy? A young couple asked me to take a photo of them, kissing as they posed against the Tuscan hills. I clicked the camera for them. 'Do you want us to take one too?' they asked me in return. 'No, thanks!' Both you and I declined the offer. You made one of your sniggering sounds. Why would we want to be dummies like everyone else? Being a tourist was already dreadful enough.

The view of the Tuscan landscape was picturesque in the soft afternoon light. You stared at the distant towns and mountains, ruminating about something. What would your parents say about our relationship? You told them a little bit about me but far from the whole story. Would you one day feel regret about us being married? And how would you take to the role as a father?

As we were leaving, I reached out my hand and touched one of the skinny oak trees, rooted on top of the tower. It trembled in the cruel wind as if it were trying to speak to me. I was disappointed by the sight of it. The tourist guide said these oaks were supposed to be old and even ancient, but in reality they were just skinny young oaks, struggling to stay rooted on top of a vicious tower. They needed real roots, real soil, real ground! I could hear their screaming and cries in the wind.

An Unknown Language

The murmuring mass of an unknown language constitutes a delicious protection . . .
Here I am protected against stupidity, vulgarity, vanity, worldliness, nationality, normality.

—Roland Barthes

The unknown language around me. The murmuring mass around me. Except that this was not a murmuring mass in Japan, this was a loud mass in Italy. This language was not too foreign for you, and you could make out many words, especially from food menus. But it was foreign for me. Even though this culture uses the same twenty-six Latin letters, just like most European languages – the same alphabet. But I didn't come from this alphabet. I came from the non-alphabetic. I came from ideograms. I came from 50,000 characters. Each character is composed with many symbols and strokes, like a tangled forest of meanings.

Also, I didn't feel this 'delicious protection' that Barthes felt. The only protection for me would be to really try to *understand* the foreign language. So that I, a secondary citizen in a white European world, would not downgrade into a tertiary citizen. But I knew that even if one day I could master a foreign language – one of the major European languages – I would still not become a primary citizen of the West.

Rome

— All the old temples in Rome, for me, somehow, are not as memorable as those vigorous flowers.
— Don't say that in front of the Romans!

We had been to Rome before, separately. But we held different ideas about the city. Maybe I was a hopeless peasant, but the first things that attracted me to a place were not historical sights, but its landscape and plants.

For me Rome was not the Colosseum or the Vatican, but the pink oleander buds in the spring wind. They were everywhere. They had not bloomed yet but one could expect they would bloom in one night with a warm breeze. The sight of those robust plants with slender leaves under the blue sky made me nostalgic for my childhood. I associated the oleander flowers with south China. They thrive in hot weather and are evergreen. In the province where I grew up, we had no winters. So the trees were green for eternity. And those oleanders, clustered together with heavy large flowers in deep December. Even though we children were constantly told that the big flowers were toxic, we still picked them and decorated our braids with them. I remember holding a little flowering branch tightly in my hand and waiting to see how they could poison me. Would they turn my fingers yellow or purple? Would I faint and die the next day? But nothing happened. As I walked home from school, the sight of butterflies dancing on the pink blooms confirmed my disbelief in their danger.

'I don't know much about tropical flowers. I'm pretty good with ferns and gum trees. I'm an expert on ivy and I love elderflowers. But that's about it.'

'But you're a landscape architect!'

'We all have our limitations. I have a love of desert land-scapes. I prefer rocks, to be honest,' you said, while we walked along the Tiber River.

'Anyway, oleanders for me are like elderflowers for you. Though you cannot make them into drinks. Do you remember the famous Van Gogh painting, the one of the vase of oleanders?'

You thought for a moment, and dragged your hand through your hair.

'You will recognise it when you see it,' I said. 'I read some-where that Van Gogh thought the flowers *joyous* and *life-affirming*. I feel the same. All the old temples in Rome, for me, somehow, are not as memorable as those vigorous flowers.'

'Don't say that in front of the Romans!' you laughed. 'They won't like to hear that their dead ruins aren't life-affirming!'

Cabin Fever

— I'm going to Lea Valley. To work on site. I can't stand this cabin fever!
— What cabin fever?
— Cabin fever is when you can't stand the confinement of indoor life! Ich kann Lagerkoller nicht ausstehen!

The honeymoon finished quickly and I felt our *die Hochzeitsreise* really had begun. *Die Hochzeitsreise* – the marriage journey. Germans seem to be much more sober and philosophical about the nature of marriage.

We had temporarily moved into a new flat in Bethnal Green. The rent was reasonable. The flat didn't have a balcony or a garden but it was warm and bright, and felt secure. We could smell curry through our neighbours' windows and walls. We could also tell which TV channel they were watching. Very frequently, I heard kids playing in the yard or babies crying, reminding me of my pregnancy and what was to come in my life.

Since you were a freelancer, you were spending most of your time at home. You moved around the small flat restlessly like a caged animal. Was it because of our excessive coffee drinking? Unlike living on the boat, we now had an unlimited supply of gas and electricity. We kept on making coffee and tea, gulping down the warm liquid. It was clear that you missed the boat life, the outdoor life. Perhaps you were not a man made for the indoors. One morning, you woke up at six. By seven thirty you said:

'I've gotta make tracks.' Registering my blank look, you added: 'You know, making tracks! *Wo zou le!* Leaving! *Ich gehe fort!*'

'Oh, where are you going?'

'I'm going to Lea Valley. To work on site. I can't stand this cabin fever!'

'What cabin fever?' I had never heard this expression before.

'Cabin fever is when you can't stand the confinement of indoor life.' You raised your voice: '*Ich kann Lagerkoller nicht ausstehen!*'

Oh! What a revelation. How long did it take to really know someone? I asked myself. I should have realised this when I first met you, when you were picking the elderflowers in the park. How could a romantic love last if our vision of life was incompatible? But then romantic love exists only because one has illusions about the other. Though maybe this was the final illusion, that love could survive the dispelling of all one's illusions about the other.

Niedersächsische Bauernhaus

– You know I want to live with you, but not in a flat.
I want to live in a Bauernhaus.
– A Bauhaus?
– Not a Bauhaus, a Bauernhaus.

'I'm sorry, but I don't think I want to live in this flat for very long,' you announced one evening, during our dumpling supper.

Somehow I had expected this. But still, it was hard for me to take when it came. I felt a shock. Then a feeling of deep hurt welled up.

'So, where do you want to live?'

'You know I want to live with you, but not in a flat. I've been thinking about it for a while and I want to live in a *Bauernhaus.*'

'A Bauhaus?'

'Not a Bauhaus, a *Bauernhaus*. A farmhouse, with woods or some outdoor space.'

You stopped eating and put down your glass. Then you said, your voice full of nostalgia, which I hated:

'When my family left Australia for Germany, we lived in a Lower Saxon farmhouse. A timber-framed brown house from my father's family. We had animals, and a few pear and apple trees. I also had my little shed my father and I built together.

It's a pity we sold it. Now that we have a baby on the way, I often think of that farmhouse . . .'

Should I support your fantasy? We lived in London, the most expensive city in Europe, and your salary barely covered our rent. You knew that I felt the need to make a family in the West. The need to put down roots. But the big decision had to be made: where were we going to live? In Britain? In Germany? Back in China? How would we sustain ourselves? We lived in a state of indecision. And I had to finish my studies before the birth. I was very anxious, and the pregnancy hormones were making it worse.

Transplant

*– I read that in China, people would transplant large
numbers of trees and bring them to the newly developed
cities. Chinese people seem to be very adaptable, like
their trees!*

*– Yes, but once the trees grow older, you can't transplant
them again. The roots are too embedded into the
ground.*

It was a strange and important trip, completely different from
all the other trips in my life. It was a trip not for me, but for
us and for our future child. In June, we flew to Berlin, and
made our way on the S-Bahn to the Pankow area, where we
could see a lake called Weißensee – the White Lake. I thought
about the fact that your family had left the southern hemisphere for a Lower Saxon farmhouse in Germany, and now
relocated again to a modern apartment in Berlin. Where
would you place your nostalgia, your *heimweh*, your
sehnsucht?

'If you don't feel comfortable, you don't have to come, you
know.' You said this before I had decided to come with you to
Germany.

But how could I not come? I had our child growing in my
body, and you and your family would be my only family in the
West. Even though we had not yet told them that we were
married. But perhaps now was a good time to tell them? This

child would not be a rootless individual like me. She would feel at home here, either in Britain or in Germany. I wanted your parents to be included in our life.

Transplant – the word you liked to use in your work. It was also my word. But then, when I thought of *transplanting* myself to Germany – where your family was – I felt goose bumps rising on my neck. *Ich bin eine Chinesisch. Ich bin eine Asiatische.* It was the same feeling I had when I first got to Britain. How many times could one restart a life?

'I read that in China, people would transplant large numbers of trees and bring them to the newly developed cities. Chinese people seem to be very adaptable, like their trees!' You were trying to comfort me.

'Yes, but once the trees grow older, you can't transplant them again. The roots are too embedded into the ground.'

We arrived at a top-floor apartment in an ornate residential building. Your mother came out to the staircase to welcome us. She had an English accent which I instantly recognised. You and she had similar cheeks, and similar smiles. Your father, a native German, was preparing food in the kitchen. I could smell the mix of melted butter and baking. The air felt warm and thick when we entered the sitting room. A chandelier glistered above our heads. Suddenly I felt I was in a European home, which I hadn't felt in any London house. But then how many London houses had I been in during my brief life in the West?

There was a large glass door onto the balcony through which one could step out to view the lake. I was overwhelmed by mixed feelings of excitement and anxiety. The high ceilings, the polished oak furniture, the classical music playing on the stereo, the armchairs with embroidered cushions, all this told me one thing – that your class was higher than my class. I was not sure exactly what your class was, but I knew what I came from – Chinese peasant stock originally, even though I had received a scholarship from Europe and I could speak two languages.

'Which part of China are you from?' your mother asked, already cutting a slice of home-made carrot cake for you and me.

'Zhejiang Province, it is below Shanghai, by the East China Sea.'

'And your parents still live there?'

'No, they died.'

'Oh, I'm so sorry.' Your mother was surprised, but she refrained from asking more questions.

I looked at my carrot cake, and took a bite. There were walnuts in it. I liked walnuts. At the same time, I was astonished that you hadn't told your family that my parents were dead. Too morbid to talk about, perhaps? For Chinese people, this would be the first information one would share. So what *had* you told them about me?

Moin

– *There we say* Moin *instead of* Guten Morgen. *And we produce the best* Würstchen im Schlafrock *in Germany.*
– *So it's like we say* have you eaten? *instead of* how are you? *in our home town.*

Almost everything in this apartment was pleasant. I sat in a soft armchair and ate what was offered to me. I studied the bookshelves and looked through the music collections. This was a different type of family home from mine. In my parents' house, very few objects were to do with the idea of leisure. Here, it seemed that there was room to think. There may even be money to spare.

Your father came to me with a cup of coffee. With a blue T-shirt and black trousers, the way he dressed was simple and modest, like a proper engineer would have done.

'Did you grow up in Germany?' I asked.

'Yes. I grew up in the north, a harbour city called Bremen. You know Bremen?'

I shook my head.

'There we say *Moin* instead of *Guten Morgen*. And we produce the best *Würstchen im Schlafrock* in Germany,' your father explained with a laugh.

I didn't know what *Würstchen im Schlafrock* was, but I could remember seeing a picture of a sausage smeared in yellow mustard at the airport. And on that picture there was a word – *Würstchen*. So I could only guess it was some sort of sausage. Maybe a very special sausage from Bremen?

'So it's like we say *have you eaten?* instead of *how are you?* in my home town.'

Everyone laughed. Then your father resumed his speech.

'But I hated Bremen, and didn't like Germany. I could not stand the sight of it, walking down my street each day, looking into everyone's garden – trimmed lawns decorated with depressing frog statues. *Trübselig!* You know this word *trübselig?* Very boring. So after college, I left for Australia! I was interested in seeing the world, especially the southern hemisphere. And I could grow my hair there, like a hippy!'

I smiled. Your father seemed to be a straightforward person, at least very direct. Every word he delivered was with precision and clarity, and with a bit of a German accent.

'You really were a hippy when I first met you!' Your mother added: 'I'll never forget the bunch of people you were travelling with, camping together in the bush near Perth.'

Your father shook his head ironically. The same irony I recognised from your face. I thought, this is interesting. Is this going to pass on to our child too?

'So why did you come back to Germany?' I enquired, eating another piece of cake.

Your father lowered his eyes and he seemed to be searching for some logical answer, like a proper elderly German man. But your mother broke in:

'One can't be a hippy for all one's life. And we both missed Europe. So he returned for an engineering job in Germany and I was able to visit my family in England more frequently.'

The conversation continued, but more between your parents. They switched to German at one point. I felt now that just by observing your parents I could unlock some secret about you, the way you were wired. But then you shifted back to English suddenly and I was jolted out of my thoughts:

'We didn't want to have a wedding now. Because she's still studying and we want to wait until she finishes. So we just went to a registry office in London before we came.'

'Oh.'

Your parents fell silent. They both looked at us and then at each other. Your father was the first to speak but he spoke in German. You all talked in German for a bit. I heard a few words like '*ja, ja, ja*' followed by a sharp inhalation from your father. And your mother was nodding her head slowly. The situation seemed to be improving. Your mother even began to smile. But at that moment my stomach tightened, a wave of nausea came up to my throat. I got up from the chair apologetically, and walked towards the bathroom as calmly as I could.

Second Trimester

- *I read that most women feel energised in their second trimester.*
- *You read that? What else did you read?*
- *Well, apparently at this stage, your uterus can expand up to twenty times its normal size. Scary if I try to visualise it.*

Among the dusty old LPs on the shelves in your parents' living room, I found a Scorpions' album with one of my favourite songs: 'Wind of Change'. I slid it onto the record player. The ever-familiar line came out: '*An August summer night / Soldiers passing by / Listening to the wind of change . . .*' So many times I had listened to this song at university, until one day an English professor told us it was anti-Communist. We students were all surprised, as we had never thought it was a song with such an evil intention. Could we still love the beautiful song without agreeing with it politically? I had not listened to it since. And now it suddenly made complete sense. The wind of change. We were in Germany – the Federal Republic of Germany, the strongest economy in Europe – and right now, in Berlin, where the wall had been removed. There were only a few remaining parts left in the city for Chinese tourists to take selfies.

You watched me humming along, and smiled.

'I didn't realise you know the Scorpions!'

Then your parents came back from the local Biomarkt with the shopping. When they heard the music playing, your father instantly sang along with his funny croaky voice:

The future's in the air
I can feel it everywhere
Blowing with the wind of change.

You and your mother laughed. I thought to myself: this is something I could never share with my own parents. They would never truly understand why I had wanted to leave China, even if they had heard of the Berlin Wall or Western rock music. And even though I missed them, quietly but miserably, they had now gone. They had disappeared into history. Yet I was still here, in the happening of history, listening to the same music with my new parents-in-law.

I could now see that you were your mother's boy. Luckily, it wasn't quite the same relationship as between Barthes and his mother. But you had inherited a lot from her. Her Englishness, her reticence, her phrases such as 'I wouldn't mind that', or 'I'm not too fond of the colour arrangement in this design' – all this had constructed your character. You father spoke much more directly, and was not a vegetarian. I wondered how long this eating separation in the same house had existed, and if your mother and father had other fundamental different views about the world. 'I don't want to see a dead animal on my kitchen table,' you always said in London while I was cooking meat. But here, you seemed to be oblivious to your father cutting up lamp chops. Perhaps that's because you were 'at home' and everyone behaved in a mutually-agreed manner.

But this time, lamb chops didn't seduce me at all. The pregnancy made me oversensitive to the smell of meat. I tried to hide my nausea.

'Are you also becoming a vegetarian?' Your mother smiled encouragingly.

You glanced at me. We had agreed that we would not say anything to them before the third trimester arrived.

I nodded, reaching for the potato salad. Now your father was left alone to eat the lamb. I could see he enjoyed the flesh greatly, along with his Berliner Kindl Weisse. I thought your mother must have guessed that I might be pregnant. But they kept cool, not imposing anything like a Chinese family would. Most of the time they left us alone.

The weather was beautiful – blue and fresh. You took me to the Weißensee. You said we must swim in the lake – your favourite activity in Berlin.

'Come on, you should do more exercise before you get too big to move!'

'But the water is cold.' I tested it with my finger. 'Are you sure this is not going to freeze the baby? Should I not be careful during my second trimester!'

'I read that most women feel energised in their second trimester.'

'You read that? What else did you read?' I teased.

'Well, apparently, at this stage your uterus can expand up to twenty times its normal size. Scary if I try to visualise it.'

Yes, it was unthinkable. But it was even more unthinkable that the baby would eventually grow so large and would need to get out from my body. Nobody could know exactly how it felt unless she had experienced it physically. Was I looking forward to that moment? Yes, but I trembled with fear.

You persuaded me to swim, and took off your shirt. After watching a few brave locals jump into the water, I changed into my swimsuit.

'Do you think your parents are a bit upset that we just got married without telling them?'

'Yes, a bit. But I think they're okay with it.'

You swam away into the distance, leaving me in the shallows. I stood in the cold, silky water, and thought, what is this? Am I being baptised? Perhaps I had been baptised into your culture and your landscape, with your family's subtle but powerful persuasion.

Real Love – Wahre Liebe

– *Once love is brought down to earth, and weighed, it's over. It's dead.*
– *But don't you agree that real love is the love that's brought down to earth? It's only real when it's mixed up with dirt and sweat. Otherwise, it's just for puppies and adolescents!*

After spending the weekend with your parents, we went to the Pergamon Museum on Monday morning. There was an exhibition of crafted rugs from the Middle East and Asia.

'It's not an exhibition I would normally go to,' you said, 'but at least you can see the scale of the museum.'

You led me through the Babylon Gates (quite impressive), and the remaining ancient European relics (less impressive I must admit), and took us upstairs to the exhibition.

I stood in front of a large piece – it was perhaps the biggest wall rug I had ever seen. It was entitled *50kg of Eternal Love*. The label explained that it was the heaviest handmade Persian rug the collectors had ever found. The flowery patterns were elaborate with three distinctive colours: red, brown and blue. And all the rectangles, octagon and circles were also woven with different shades of red, brown and blue.

I loved what was hanging in front of me, and tried to get you to see it. But you were not impressed.

'Well, you can't measure love,' you said.

'For a non-romantic, that is a very romantic thing to say,' I replied, imitating your sardonic way. Then I felt a bit annoyed, and continued: 'But this is not about measuring love!'

'So, the title is a joke? This must have been a love affair at its end. Once love is brought down to earth, and weighed, it's over. It's dead.'

'But don't you agree that real love is the love that's brought down to earth? It's only real when it's mixed up with dirt and sweat. Otherwise, it's just for puppies and adolescents!'

You looked at me, then suddenly produced a line I had heard somewhere before:'I think we will have to agree to disagree.'

I was speechless. I now understood what this line meant. I had not understood it when my professor spoke the same sentence before.

'Look, I prefer this one.' You pointed to the piece that was now in front of you. It was a colourful rug with extremely busy patterns of leaves and flowers, titled *Die Organisation des chaotischen Geistes* – the Organisation of a Chaotic Mind. An interesting title for a rug, as far as I was concerned. All the patterns showed a perfect picture of mess. But the mess stopped by the margin of the rug, as if expressing the fact that the material rules the mental.

The Organisation of a Chaotic Mind, I murmured to myself. It was exactly how I felt about my life now – the PhD research, the rented London home, my life with you, and our future child. But I could only organise details and patterns of daily tasks in order to move to the next stage. My thoughts remained chaotic.

Superstitious

– Well, I hope she won't turn out to be some monster.
– Shush! Don't squawk like a crow. I am superstitious
about these things!

Our flight back to London was on a Tuesday night. I was surprised to find out that you had arranged a gynaecologist appointment for me before we left.

'Why? Don't we have the NHS in England?' I asked, when the taxi dropped us in front of a building with a sign: *MD M. Roos, Facharzt für Gynäkologie und Geburtenhilfe.*

'Yes. But we might have to wait for a few weeks to be seen in London. In any case it's good to have a German doctor to examine you. So we have a second opinion.' You then pressed the doorbell.

In the quiet, white reception room, you read today's *Tagesspiegel.* My hand rested on my belly as I waited anxiously. I could feel the foetus moving actively.

The gynaecologist was a man in his late forties. He spoke a mix of German and English to me in your presence. He scanned my stomach, informing me everything was in good order. Then he paused a bit with his ultrasound machine, and looked at the monitor carefully.

'Ah, so it is *she*,' the doctor said: '*Ein Mädchen!*'

We looked at each other. This was a real surprise. When we were in London we told our doctor not to tell us the sex of the baby.

'Are you sure?' you asked.

'Yes, I think so,' he said, taking another look at the monitor. '*Es ist ein Mädchen.*'

I looked up at the monitor. But the image was so blurry, it was almost impossible for me to make sense of what was what.

On the way from the clinic to the airport, we sat in the taxi, studying a scan of the foetus – our supposed baby girl at the gestational age of twenty weeks. The black-and-white picture looked odd – a rough resemblance to a future human. Her tiny body was already formed, with limbs. Even the toes were visible. Her legs were tightly hugging her upper body like a cave-dwelling creature. Though there were no facial details (did I see her eyelids or was it just my imagination?) her head seemed to be quite large compared with her other body parts.

'Her big head must be from you, since I have a small head,' I said to you.

'Well, I hope she won't turn out to be some monster.'

'Shush! Don't squawk like a crow. I am superstitious about these things!'

When we arrived at the airport, the picture was worn out. It was almost torn apart by our excessive study.

A Perfect Reproduction

> – *What is the difference between a perfect reproduction*
> *and an original?*
> – *There is no intrinsic difference between the perfect repro-*
> *duction and the original. The only difference is the exter-*
> *ior difference, and that is to do with its history.*

So this was it, I told myself. Nearly three years of PhD research and writing would come to an end, and after that I would be free. But free for what, though? For motherhood? For a woman's role in the house and outside the house?

The examination committee was made up of three people. My supervisor Grant was not included in the viva, as is standard procedure. I had met two of the examiners before, and the external supervisor was from the University of Manchester. Was I nervous during the whole session? Yes. And being six and a half months pregnant added to the stress level. Of course the professors didn't stare at my belly, which was not that obvious under my loose shirt.

I gave an outline of my thesis; the committee proceeded with their questions. I tried to deliver my answers as well as I could. The external examiner had some concerns.

'In your thesis you quote extensively from Walter Benjamin's "The Work of Art in the Age of Mechanic Reproduction".' The professor from Manchester leafed through my thick pages. 'It's interesting you suggest that Chinese labourers are the new mechanics to serve the reproduction, and that the art world has been transformed by this no-authorship industry. But I'm not convinced that you have understood that Benjamin wrote this essay in the early 1930s. He was in a desperate state, running away from Nazi Germany. His attitude towards the age of mechanical reproduction was ambiguous and complex, yet in your essay you don't bring in any of that historical background.'

I stared at the professor who was speaking, sweat dripping down from my neck. Damn it, the Jewish/Nazi thing again – how could a Chinese person ever hope to get it right? This kind of mistake could be made only by someone like me – someone neither from a European background nor interested in analysing everything from a Western point of view.

'Also, I am not entirely sure of your argument on fake and real.' He leafed through my pages again.

At this point, another supervisor from the committee came to his help and found the passage:

'. . . *the argument of fake or real is a by-product of the copyright industry in the West. As long as the global market based on slavery – and on such a large quantity of Chinese labourers – continues to produce the products for world consumers, there will be no such thing as a "fake" or "genuine". For example, all Mac computers are either made or assembled in China by the hands of cheap labourers. What is an original, and what is a copy? All fakes are real, as the so-called "quality control" and "intellectual property" are based on power and slavery, as Western democracy is also based on power and slavery . . .'*

Now the third supervisor looked at me above his reading glasses, slightly alarmed. Before I could defend myself, he remarked:

'What I don't understand is why the fact that products are manufactured in a system of wage slavery means we cannot talk of "genuine" as opposed to "fake". After all, a genuine Mac is just a Mac produced under certain conditions, legal and physical, which involve wage slavery. The presence of slavery does not mean we can no longer talk of "fake" as opposed to "genuine". The same holds for paintings. If slaves had been part of Modigliani's or da Vinci's atelier then would that mean there were no genuine Modiglianis or da Vincis?'

I was suddenly flummoxed. Before I could respond, he continued:

'But Benjamin suggested art is reproducible. So if that was the case, what is the difference between a perfect reproduction and an original?' The professor from Manchester paused and glanced at me.

I thought I was having a panic attack. I could not continue this. My mind was a chaotic place, and there was no organisation to it. My body was not helping either, and my stomach cramped. I felt like vomiting. All I could remember was that I managed to say:

'There is no intrinsic difference between the perfect reproduction and the original. The only difference is the exterior difference, and that is to do with its history.'

I went on to answer more questions, but I didn't know what I was saying. After the discussion, I was asked to leave the room for some moments. Staggering, I made my way to the bathroom. Alone, in front of a mirror, I saw a ghostly pale-looking woman. My vision dissolved into blankness. My sugar level was going down. I sat on the toilet, faintly, and swallowed a piece of chocolate. I must recover. The committee must have sensed my fragile state. Perhaps they would take mercy on me, and give me another chance? In the seminar room, I hadn't wanted to explain that my nausea was a result of my pregnancy. It would be very unprofessional. And they were men. Men! After waiting in the lobby for about twenty minutes – it felt like a century – I was called back in. I was informed that I had successfully passed the viva. Passed? Did I mishear? I stared at everyone, and they were all smiling, nodding, confirming, as if I was the Virgin on the Rocks. But I had thought they'd wanted to fail me! I knew that examiners could be critical, but *that* critical? Or was it just my high oestrogen levels, a pregnant woman's oversensitivity?

I knew that my essay was not the greatest thesis ever written. Still, it had some kernels of originality in it, even though the examiners didn't seem to be very interested in my main argument. What was my main argument? Already it was beginning to fade from my mind. The idea was that slavery was at the heart of a capitalistic system where reproduction was the main engine. All the things I wrote about originality were kind of beside the point. Originality is a fetish of people who want to control the art market and the publishing industry. It's also a fetish of academics, particularly the males and old farts. What I was really interested in – though right then even this was blurring in my mind – were the sweating workers in Chinese villages. It was their lives, their anonymity, their way of looking at Western classics, and their purely pragmatic attitude. I loved being with those artisans and feeling their energy and their lack of self-consciousness. They were not precious in any way about their work, or about their life. But they were full of heart, and at the same time they were not clinging to their achievements. They were part of the flow of life. I had come from the same culture, and I felt I could not make this clear or make Westerners understand. The Western language and mentality did not allow me to do it.

流水不腐 – *liu shui bu fu*

- *In Chinese, we say* liu shui bu fu – *flowing water does not rot. If the water does not flow, it is dead water. It will rot.*
- *Water does not rot or die. It can be polluted or stagnant, but the water itself is always water. It's just molecules.*

Something had happened to the lock-keeper's cottage. I was passing one day and noticed building work. It was scaffolded. At first I thought they were destroying the house. Really? Were they knocking down my favourite house in this country? My heart was in my throat, and I jumped onto a pile of rubble in front of the house and got as close as I could. Through the dusty scaffolding, I could see inside. It seemed to be reconstructed. No. It would be called a *renovation*. Two builders each stood on a ladder, drilling and hammering. The noise was unbearable.

I found myself on my bench beside the cottage. The nasturtium bushes were no longer there, nor the dead sunflowers. Instead, there was a pile of cement on the ground. And the lock-keeper's cottage was no longer a cottage. I could see a brand-new second floor being added, with big shiny windows reflecting the sky. The brick walls of the old part of the house still remained a rusty brown, but the new part was painted black. It squatted on the old cottage like an

224

evil bird. A *For Sale* sign had been erected in front of the house. A few cyclists passed, paying no attention to the new building.

There were masses of dandelion seeds floating on the canal, mixed with a thick layer of duckweeds. The water was not moving at all. It was like a piece of patterned marble, imposing itself in front of me.

'The canal water is dead,' I once said to you, when we were still living our boat life.

'What do you mean?'

'In Chinese, we say *liu shui bu fu* – flowing water does not rot. If the water does not flow, it is dead water. It will rot.'

You didn't agree: 'That sounds a bit weird in English. Water does not rot or die. It can be polluted or stagnant, but the water itself is always water. It's just molecules.'

That's a very scientific way of thinking about water. You didn't see the life and death in water. That's just like saying a rainbow is only a spectrum.

If we had some money, we could have bought the lock-keeper's cottage. I could get up and stand by the window upstairs, drinking coffee and watching the water flow before leaving for the day. And I would catch sight of night falling after I came home from work. Well, the work that I hoped for was still in the future. I felt a cramp in my womb. Another cramp. I would have to wait a while before using my PhD. I stretched my legs. The large cotton skirt I was wearing fit tightly around my swollen belly. It was loose on me two months ago, but not now. The fabric had been stretched and I could see two threads hanging loose, from a ripped seam at the waist.

EIGHT

右

RIGHT

Skin to Skin

*— Touch her and bring her close to your breasts. Skin to
skin. So that your hormones will respond and stimulate
the milk.*

Lying on an operating table, I was under a local anaesthetic
reaching up to my chest. My head was clear, but it swelled up
with inexplicable fear while the nurses prepared for the surgery around me. You sat beside me, trying to look as calm as
you could. But your hand gripped my hand so tight that it
almost hurt. The information I received was that the baby was
in the breech position. And, I had a low-lying placenta.
Caesarean section was necessary. The doctors were dealing
with the machines around me. I could sense some frightful
movements were going on in the lower part of my body but I
could not feel anything. No, I felt nothing, not physically.
There was a curtain blocking my view. So I could not see anything but I could hear everything. What was going on? Were
they actually opening me up now? Metal tools hitting a table.
The sound of scissors cutting something. A machine beeping.

I closed my eyes, and I visualised a scene where my lower
body had been cut open: two hands (but not mine) pulled out
the baby. Then suddenly I heard a woman's voice:

'Here she is!'

What was that? Was that my mother speaking? I opened
my eyes, petrified. No. I saw nothing. Only the white medical
curtain and your anxious face.

'What a lovely girl!' Another woman's voice.

A lovely girl? Was she out? Or was I hallucinating?

No, this was not a hallucination from the anaesthetic. It was real. Something had just happened. But why did I not hear crying? Was the baby alive?

At first the baby did not cry. And they didn't give her to me immediately. But I understood she must be out of my body now, because I saw you standing up and moving towards where the action was. Someone must have been holding the baby, perhaps one of the nurses? Then they inserted some device into my womb. Something alien. Were they trying to suck up the placenta? The equipment was causing my chest to heave and throb violently. A strong pressure had come up through my body and I was freaking out. I began to yell. They paused the sucking machine for a bit, perhaps to check if I was okay. But after a few seconds it started again. Then the throbbing finished and I was lying on my back hearing my baby cry.

Yes, it was the cry of a newborn – bawling. It was very different from any other cry I had ever heard in my life.

'Is she okay? Can I see her?' I begged, feeling totally out of my body.

'Yes, she is fine. Don't worry.'

I heard your voice speaking somewhere near me. Then you added:

'They are just checking the baby, weighing her.'

Suddenly someone (was it you or a nurse?) laid the baby on my chest, and told me to hold it. This was a very strange moment, impossible to describe. There she was, this tiny human, eyes closed and hair wet, lying on my chest and bawling in a loud voice. Her umbilical cord was cut and clamped with a strange knot hanging down from her small belly. Did the cutting hurt the baby? I wondered. What if they left the cord uncut? Could she survive?

'Touch her and bring her close to your breasts. Skin to skin.' A woman's voice said. 'So that your hormones will respond and stimulate the milk.'

Skin to skin. Yes. I did instantly as I was told. But how would my hormones make the milk come? This sounded scientific but also enigmatic. I latched the little wrinkly wet face onto my breast, as if I knew what to do. But I had no idea what to do. The images from movies didn't come to me at that moment, I was merely reacting to the real. Yes, the real. Overwhelming, beyond thoughts. The nurses were now busy gathering around my lower body. They must have been stitching me up. Suddenly I noticed a bucket under my table. I stopped myself from looking inside.

Original and Original Copy

*– Would you like to have an original certificate? Or to
have an original copy as well?*

*– An original and an original copy? You mean, they are
both original? Even the copy?*

A month or so after the birth, I felt I was slowly recovering.
The pain from the incision still hurt every day, even after taking painkillers, but I felt I was almost human. I could be a
dignified woman again, rather than a sow that had just finished producing piglets.

What came with the newborn was a little red book. I took
a look at the little red book. Inside was a record of the newborn's hospital number, birthday, weight, mother's name and
birthday, the baby's future vaccination dates, the health visi-
tor's contact details and so on. There was also a leaflet, informing us that we had forty-two days to register the child with the
local authority. Did that mean we would then receive a birth
certificate after the registration? I asked myself. I had never
done anyone's birth certificate in my life, and didn't know that
I would not immediately receive a certificate right after the
birth. How unnatural. Now weeks had passed, and we had less
than ten days to register her.

As a privileged white European, owning more than one
passport, you had more knowledge about nationalities than
me. In the waiting room, you said:

'The baby will be British automatically, because I have multiple citizenship. But that means she can't have your nationality. She can't be Chinese.'

I looked at you with blurry eyes. That's right. The Chinese government didn't allow dual nationalities. But still, emotionally, I found it difficult to accept. How did I end up producing an English child? Given that neither of us was English! Then I looked around. A few families with newborns in their prams were also waiting to be registered. Among all the straight-looking, same-race couples, there was a white woman with a brown-skinned man, a white man with a dark-coloured woman, and two women with a child. All sorts. Did they have similar problems to the one I had? I pulled back my gaze and looked at our baby sleeping in the pram – she looked neither Chinese nor European. Her face was still wrinkled, red, like the face of a strange, tiny, hairless old man.

Finally, our number was called and we were received by a registrar. This was the first time I had physically (not just mentally) experienced this word: multiculturalism. On all levels.

A dark-skinned man in his early fifties smiled warmly at us. The name tag on his blue shirt said: *Mr Mustafa Abdo, Senior Civil Servant (G5).*

Mr Abdo shook our hands. He teased the sleeping baby with his index finger (touching her left cheek gently) to show his friendliness. He then sat down, typing our details on his computer. His accent was Ghanaian or perhaps Nigerian? To my surprise, the whole registration process was simple, no fuss, no complications at all. Perhaps it was because we had presented our brand-new marriage certificate, despite your having said that this piece of paper was not relevant here.

Maybe you were right. Mr Abdo didn't seem to be particularly interested in the actual father of the child. He didn't even look at you properly. He just asked for your birth date and your nationality, whether or not you had a middle name. He then took only a brief glance at your passport – it could have been anyone who resembled you. I could not help but think about how the registration process would be in China – what would the Communist Party do if the father was a non-Chinese?

The only puzzling moment came at the end. Mr Abdo finished off his typing and printed out the forms. He asked:

'Would you like to have just the original certificate? Or do you want to have an original copy as well?' Then he added: 'An original copy costs an extra twenty pounds per copy.'

'An original and then an original copy?' I was confused. 'You mean, they are both originals? Even the copy?'

'Yes, the original copy I will produce here is original.' He was now looking at the printed-out paper and added: 'If you wish to order some copies in the future, then it's different. The future copies will be produced in another place.'

You winked at me. Suddenly, I remembered the examiners' questions during my viva. I might well have found the way to improve my arguments about reproduction and Walter Benjamin. The answer lay in the distinction between original and original copy, and then future copies! Mr Mustafa Abdo probably didn't need a PhD to make his point clear. He had all the answers!

Disembodiment

– *How do you feel?*
– *I feel this disembodiment. I feel half of my body has left
  me, but is still near me. And I can't really function
  with my own body alone.*

Then your parents arrived. They had brought with them many
presents for our newborn. A teddy bear, a singing turtle, a
bird mobile to hang above the crib, colourful plastic bowls
and plates, two mini dresses. Your mother even wrapped an
orange-coloured dummy in shiny paper. Each item seemed to
have a German label. Not *Made in China* at all. I noticed the
teddy bear was not new. It looked slightly moth-eaten. Your
mother pointed out: 'This is from when I was a little girl! My
mother bought it for me when we were still in England. It's
been with me ever since.' Then she squeezed the toy. 'You're
a real antique. Aren't you, Teddy!'

You looked embarrassed, then you said: 'We'd better take
care of it.'

I took the teddy in my hand, feeling weird about having
some toy from a grandmother I had never met. I felt uncomfortable with connecting myself to this unknown woman's
world. You mentioned once that your grandmother died long
ago, and that she was from Cornwall. That was all I knew. And
now, we had inherited her teddy bear, through your mother.
Somehow I never liked these things people called 'teddies'. I

had not grown up with toys. I played with earth and animals in the fields when I was young. And I always associated teddy bears with lonely housewives in the West. But I thanked your mother, for her good intentions.

Now the baby was dressed in one of the new suits your parents had bought. A pink one, with blue flowers. This was bizarre. All these German baby products fit her no matter what she looked like. A mixed-raced newborn, she didn't look very much like me, or you. Her hair was light brown, her eyes light blue with dark shades.

My wound still gave me a tearing sensation in my belly when I moved. Getting up to feed the baby or go to the toilet caused agonising pain. Your parents helped us during the day. They changed nappies and cooked. In the evening they went back to their hotel. They would only stay for a week. On the final day of their stay, we went out for dinner. After we ordered and the baby had fallen asleep in her crib, your father looked at us intently, and said:

'Do you think you will be happy staying in London? Maybe you want to try to raise the child in Germany?'

Your mother nodded in agreement and added:

'I know London is an exciting place to be. But childcare is better in Germany. Especially with what's happening now in Britain.'

You nodded, but didn't say anything. I could see you were thinking about something. I didn't make any comments. I wasn't sure what would be good for me or for the child. I had been finding it impossible to think straight after the birth. And right then in the restaurant I was feeling even more foggy.

Your parents then began to talk about different areas around Berlin, and I heard the word *Tempelhof* and *Brandenburg*. But then the baby woke up and started to cry. I brought her to my breast, losing the thread of the conversation.

The day after your parents left, I felt something was wrong. But I didn't know what. When she was here, I had felt I didn't very much like your mother's presence, but now she was gone I realised she had been helpful and sympathetic. Then I thought of your father. I liked your father. I liked his straight-forwardness and methodical way of thinking. I wished they could have stayed longer. The thought of them made me think of my dead parents. Would the scene in front of me now have been utterly unimaginable for them? If only the dead could imagine. But then I could not picture my parents at all. They had disappeared and my thoughts could no longer reach them or bring their presence back to me.

With only you and me and the baby, the days became long again with repetitive housework and childcare. Nights were worse. You didn't look as stressed as me, but you had also lost your sense of self. You were not the same person I knew before. After the baby went back to sleep, you would repeatedly ask about my feelings, as if you hadn't seen me for months.

'How do you feel?' you would ask with a disconcerted look.

'I feel the same. As I told you.'

'The same . . .' It was as if you found this answer too abstract to grasp.

'I feel this disembodiment. I feel half of my body has left me, but is still near me. Or staying next to me. And I can't really function with my own body alone.'

'Disembodiment.' You thought about this for a moment, then said: 'Maybe there is negative disembodiment and positive disembodiment. I hope it will become positive disembodiment for you.'

'How can there be a positive disembodiment?' I objected, while trying to sit up and pump milk from my breast with a pumping machine. It hurt terribly. 'For a man, it's really impossible to know what it's like,' I said. 'Try to imagine you are me – part of your own body is now outside in the world.' I tried to describe the sensation in between the motion of the breast pumps. 'It is hard to get used to the idea of part of your own flesh gaining its own life and having left you.'

'You will adjust. I am sure,' you remarked, quite casually, as if you suddenly got the whole process. You went to open the fridge. You needed a beer, that's what you needed after a whole day with the baby. Then you sank into the sofa, with your beer and your newspaper.

Regression / Progression

– Oh, regression! She stopped talking!
– Well, she seemed to respond to singing.

The small life inside the onesie was growing – a bundle of activity and softness, like a crab inside a shell.

'I wish we could wear onesies too, they're much better than jeans. And warm.'

'Why don't you?' I responded, lifting the baby's tiny arms and marshmallow legs into the onesie and buttoning it up.

Every day she was different from the day before. We noticed that the baby seemed to make a sound like 'hello' at four months, or were we just imagining that she had managed to utter something sensible beyond all senselessness? Staring into space with shining eyes, smiling, she would mimic the two syllables: He-Loo. You would kneel on our futon bed, facing her and encouraging her to keep saying hello. He-Loo, the little bundle repeated. Then you tried 'how are you' and it seemed the baby was sensitive to speech expression. Whoo-ooo-yuu, she muttered. I thought there would be progress from then on, but weeks later she stopped trying to 'talk' and just made coos and squawks.

'Oh, regression! She stopped talking!' I said.

'Well, she seems to respond to singing.' You carried her in your arms and hummed a little tune.

I thought I could hear you murmuring '*your own personal Jesus . . .*' – that song Johnny Cash once sang. I could feel that you wanted the baby to make progress as much as I did.

In the fifth month, we trained her to turn over on the bed by herself. She seemed to be able to kick herself over, flipping from her back to her tummy and then back again. But a week later, she stopped doing it, and she would lie on her stomach for ages, raising her neck and crying, unable to flip.

'Oh, poor thing. Maybe she doesn't have a strong enough neck, and her arm muscles are too weak to turn herself over.'

'But I don't understand this regression.' You observed her on the bed like a scientist scrutinising a white rat in an experiment. 'It was clearly a new development last week. How come she can't remember how to flip any more?'

I listened, and wondered why we were so anxious about progress. Was it that we didn't trust nature? Or that we just wanted to control life to make ourselves feel safe and better?

The Taste of Your Milk

– I don't really like the taste of your milk. Too sweet.
– That's insulting. But the baby likes it!

Time passed. The newborn grew into a six-month-old. You returned to your work routine and I tried to stop breastfeeding at night. But the plan was too intellectual for my body, and for the baby. In her brief six months of life, she had always fallen asleep next to my breasts, sometimes with her mouth still attached to my nipple. Now without my nipple in her mouth, she would not sleep. Even though I bought three different types of bottle with nipple-shaped teats, she would still recognise the difference between plastic and skin flesh. Her little mouth spat out the plastic nipple the second I pushed it into her mouth. But I carried on trying, without giving in.

As soon as I reduced the frequency of the feeds, my breasts were engorged and they hurt to the point of tears.

'You have a fever, you're burning up,' you said, touching my forehead.

'It was like this last night, just the same.'

The temperature continued. My breasts turned to rocks. The milk wouldn't come out. We were up all night fretting. Early in the morning, we got up and went to see the doctor. It was only then we heard the word – mastitis.

'You must get the milk out from your breasts, otherwise it can be quite bad – the blocked ducts will be infected, then the fever will get worse,' the doctor warned me, writing a pre-scription. 'Take the antibiotics daily. And you have to use a pump to get the milk out.'

'Yes, we have one,' I said.

'Then keep using it. It will help.'

The pump didn't really work. It actually traumatised one of my breasts. It got worse. Even the baby got fed up with my inflamed nipples, her once beloved objects. In the middle of the night, in agonising pain, I woke you up.

'Please, I am so sorry, but I am in pain!' Then I stretched my upper body towards you. 'Suck me hard. It might come out if you really try.'

Wearily and slowly, you rose from the sofa bed. You had suffered the same sleep deprivation as me since we'd had the baby.

'How should I suck it?' You stared at my two engorged globes, and checked my temperature. 'Is it that bad?' You felt the rock-hard tissue with your finger.

I pulled up a chair and sat in front of you. You tried to find a good upward position to face my breasts. This had abso-lutely nothing to do with lovemaking or passion. It was a medical emergency that called for collaboration and precision from both partners. You squatted before me at an uncomfort-able angle and sucked my breasts. It was excruciating, but miraculously my milk began flowing. Once I was unblocked, the white liquid gushed down on your face. You almost choked.

'Can I stop now?' You stood up, coughing with a mouthful of milk and rubbing your knees.

Within moments I could see my breasts becoming softer, then the hard tissue turning flat. The pain gradually faded. You spat out a last bit of milk, and complained:

'I don't really like the taste of your milk. Too sweet.'

'That's insulting. But the baby likes it!'

I had never tasted my own milk. I dipped my finger in the little drops coming out of my nipple. It did taste sweet, but I wondered why you didn't like it. You loved having milk in your tea every day. Did the act of drinking human milk disgust you, because it forced you to confront the fact that we're animals, when it comes down to it?

We lay exhausted on the bed, and fell asleep with the speed of a grasshopper. The baby was still sleeping. Soon she would wake up and would cry for milk.

Hysterical

– How come you have become such a hysterical person?
– Me? Hysterical? If I am hysterical, it's you who have made me hysterical!

I had few memories of how my mother raised me during my early years. I had memories from much later, of kindergarten and primary school. All I knew was that my mother didn't want to have a big family. She didn't even want to have children. She was the oldest child in her family, and she had looked after her six younger sisters from a very early age. When she was a teenager, her parents became ill and she had to look after them too. Her mother was a tea farmer, who suffered from severe rheumatoid arthritis before she died. My mother's life bore no resemblance to the life she wanted to live. Perhaps I could understand why she didn't like having a child and having to maintain her own family. I tried to find some happy memories with my mother. A kind word, a soft smile, or a cuddle. But nothing came to my mind. I could not think of any gentle moment with the woman who had given birth to me. What did come to me was the day when our buffalo lost her unborn calf. That was before my father got a job in the town. We owned a few water buffaloes on our rice paddy. One of the buffaloes was pregnant. One afternoon my mother found the animal lying on its side, bleeding, the placental membranes hanging from the opening of the animal's vagina. I had just come home from school, and I was in my first year. I stood beside the bleeding animal, slightly frightened, but not knowing what was wrong with it. Then my mother said:

'That's good. I was hoping the calf would die. I have had enough of them.' Then she turned to look at me and added: 'I managed to abort three before you came along. I didn't manage to abort you.'

Only eight years old, I didn't understand what an abortion was. But seeing the bleeding tissues hanging down from the buffalo's lower body at that moment formed my concept of birth and death. Finally, the placenta dropped onto the ground, completely. And the buffalo struggled to stand up, letting out a low and painful grunt.

'To live is just to suffer. Nothing good comes out of it.'

My mother walked away from the animal. Bringing back a bucket of water, she washed the blood off the ground.

Now, with my own daughter in my arms, I tried to imagine how my mother had nursed me, or if indeed she had at all. But my imagination didn't get very far. The baby had had colic for the last few days and was vomiting milk after every feed. I tried lying her on her tummy and rubbing her back, or bathing her and massaging her belly. When she felt better, she would immediately cry for food. Then there was the diarrhoea. Often an explosion of poo that would seep out through her nappy, soaking her onesie. And I would scream to you while lifting her two small legs:

'Quick! Get me a wipe!'

There was no response, only the sound of Radio 4 – Melvyn Bragg's *In Our Time* – from the kitchen. But you were not in the kitchen. I could smell burnt toast.

I called again.

Still no answer. One of her legs slipped from my grip and landed firmly in her own poo. Now the poo was spreading everywhere: the bed sheet, pillow, blanket and your mum's teddy. I let the other leg go, stormed into the bathroom and grabbed the wipes. Only then did you appear with a book in your hand.

'Did you not hear me screaming?'

'No. When?'

'When? Are you sure your ears are okay?'

'I'm not deaf. What's wrong?'

'Then why can't you just hear me?!'

I wiped the brown liquid from the baby's bottom and tried to clean the sheet.

'What's that word, *heedless*. You're heedless! You prefer reading books to helping me!'

'I am not heedless.' You shrugged, watching me wipe the bed.

'Okay, you are not heedless. But if you cannot hear the screaming, you should get your ears checked!'

'Give me a break. How come you have become such a hysterical person?'

'Me? Hysterical? If I am hysterical, it's you who have made me hysterical!'

Now, at home, we talked only about buying nappies, washing sheets or visiting clinics. We no longer talked about films or books. Cultural activities seemed to belong to other people

– either rich people with nannies and servants, or childless people. Had we become a typical boring middle-class family of the kind I had loathed before I entered this state of matrimony? How could I get out of this? It was too late. So this was the club most women belonged to, and on which society built itself. It seemed to me that the whole of human life (biologically and socially) was a conspiratorial system designed against women.

Abandon

– How can you abandon me for two weeks when I am still breastfeeding?

– I am not abandoning you. I need to make a living for us.

Then you announced that you had to go to Germany for a big project. You would be joining a local team planning an organic farm. You needed to be away for two weeks.

'Two weeks? You're going to leave me and the baby here for two weeks?'

'I'll do a big shop for you before I leave: drinks, food and tons of nappies. I promise.'

'What a pile of shit. How can you abandon me for two weeks when I am still breastfeeding and can hardly sleep?'

'I'm not abandoning you. I could call my mother and ask if she'll come over to help?'

I shook my head. The thought of living with my mother-in-law in this flat scared me. I'd rather be alone.

'I'm sorry. I know two weeks is long. But I need to make a living for us. You have no income at the moment.'

You were right. But still, I'd rather be poor than be left alone with this little whining thing. This was unfair. Why is it always the woman who takes care of the child?

Then you left. I had no family in this country, and no friends. Since I had arrived here, my days were either consumed in the library or spent with you. I had not built any social network. I knew a few PhD students from my studies, but they weren't close enough to call if I felt low. They say the first-generation immigrants have the toughest survival experience, and I wondered if I had officially become a first-generation immigrant, now that I had given birth to a British child.

All day long, I stayed in my pyjamas, except for when we went out to the shops. I looked at the baby and doubts about the choices I had made swamped me. I should have chosen a career before childbearing. How stupid. And I kept asking myself: WHY THE HELL DO WOMEN DO THIS? Many do it willingly and repeatedly. Now I knew, first hand, what an effort a woman has to make just to keep a young baby alive – to keep it fed and warm, away from physical harm, meningitis or whooping cough. How utterly dependent infants are. I asked myself: how is it possible that it is so difficult to keep a child safe but so easy to kill someone? Every day when you turn on the television or open a newspaper, there are reports of killings. Men kill other men, with rage or with cold precision and detachment, en masse or one by one. Men kill without thinking about those mothers who have tried so hard to keep their children alive until the day they get shot. Women bringing humans into the world does not make the news, and their efforts are not acknowledged. What kind of world is this? I should have become a radical feminist. I should never have given birth. And I should never have brought a life into this awful world.

Brexhausted

– We are Brexhausted. Everybody has started to hoard medicines. They say some medications might run out once Britain crashes out of the EU.

You called me every day from north-west Germany. Sometimes you sent text messages too. But then for about two days, I didn't hear anything from you. I called, and your phone was out of range. I didn't know where you were. Even in a remote part of Germany, there should have been telephone signals. Were you so busy that you were not even able to write me an email? With the baby in my arms, I thought of the story of Lady Meng Jiang. A tale from two thousand years ago. Lady Meng Jiang's husband was sent by imperial officials to build the Great Wall of China. She waited for him to return, year after year. But she received no news from him. Unable to bear her lonely existence, she decided to set out to the north, taking his winter clothes with her. After the long journey she reached the Great Wall only to find her husband had already died. Lady Meng Jiang wept bitterly. She wept day and night on the Wall, her tears drenching the stones beneath her. Eventually a part of the Great Wall collapsed. Among the broken masonry and bricks, she looked down and found the bones of a man. She recognised the skeleton of her dead husband.

Well, you were away, designing an unknown great wall somewhere in Germany. And I knew I would never become a woman who would carry a child and winter clothes for you to wear. If I did not hear anything from you this afternoon, I would leave this house and leave you altogether. I cursed you in my heart, looking at my phone in one hand and clutching the baby in the other. Perhaps the curse would have some power. And then the phone rang. It was you, sounding apologetic and guilt-ridden, explaining your whereabouts and your activities. 'I was in a mining site with a group of architects and then we visited a nuclear power station. It's amazing how much I learned about the area . . .' Your voice was infused with excitement. I hung up. I was jealous of you and your ungraspable world.

And I had not told you that the baby had had an ear infection for the last few days. I was having problems getting medicines for her. Yesterday I took her to the chemist again, to see if they had the new antibiotics coming in this week. I was told that children's antibiotics were not going to be available for some days. The ladies shook their heads, sympathetically, and added:

'We are Brexhausted. Everybody has started to hoard medicines. They say some medication might run out once Britain crashes out of the EU.'

Strange, and terrible, I thought. We knew nothing of what our future would be in this country! Perhaps no one really knew what was going on, including the current prime minister herself. And the Queen wouldn't have a clue either. Apparently, she was still very much alive.

Wasteland zu Verkaufen

– I don't want to live on a wasteland!
– Don't just look at this picture. You need to have some imagination!

Then, after two weeks, you came back. But you didn't come back by yourself, you brought a hippy caravan with you. The caravan was parked outside our flat, it was red and blue but with mud up the sides. You looked so scruffy, with a beard covering your chin and cheeks. You hair was long and greasy. In your rucksack, there were stacks of documents about the land, and maps, as well as your drawings.

'How is the baby?' you asked, taking her from my arms. Your hands were cold and dirty.

'Stop! Don't give her germs! Wash your hands first!'

You returned from the bathroom, while I was looking at the van outside the window.

'You bought that?' I frowned.

'Yes, don't you like it? It was cheap, cost almost nothing.'

You took the baby and began to make faces at her. But she cried instantly, and you stopped making faces.

'What do we want with a van?' I asked. 'We live in London, we don't need it!'

'Aren't you pleased that we now have a mobile home? It can fit a king-size mattress and a cot. We can even fit a mini kitchen in if you want.'

I was speechless. First we got ourselves a boat, now a caravan. What next? I watched you making yourself coffee and toast, and there was this nervous excitement in your energy.

'Guess what.' You looked very animated and obviously couldn't wait to tell me something. 'I want to take you to see a piece of land I found. You've got to come with me to see it!'

'What the hell are you talking about? You found a piece of land?'

'Yes, it's not so great yet. It's sort of a wasteland. But it will be great, I promise! It'll be amazing! We can borrow some money and buy it! Because no one wants it – it's been a rubbish dump for years. We'll build a house on it and grow vegetables and fruit trees!'

'Where is it?'

'It's in Lower Saxony, where my father comes from.'

'But that's in Germany! I don't want to live in Germany.'

'Maybe not yet, but soon, I hope!' You brought out a stack of papers from your rucksack. 'I'll show you.'

You opened a map for me. Well, it was not really a map, more an architect's site plan. I couldn't understand what I was meant to look at. It vaguely showed a building footprint, travelways, some drainage facilities, sanitary sewer lines, water lines and some hills.

Then you opened a newspaper, and pointed to a photo. The headline: 'WASTELAND ZU VERKAUFEN', which I roughly made out as 'wasteland for sale'. The picture showed a very sad-looking mine pit with pools of dirty water, and bleak surroundings.

'This looks awful. I thought Lower Saxony was a rich place,' I said. 'I don't want to live on a wasteland!'

'Don't just look at this picture. You need to have some imagination!'

Ah, imagination. Imagination was the only thing left in my life, nothing else. No roots, no job, no career.

You swallowed hot coffee, and said with some seriousness: 'It's been my dream to find a cheap plot of land so I can do whatever I want on it. We can't do that in London, or in Berlin.'

'But you will never convince me to live on a sad, cold farm. No way. I'd go back to my tropical Chinese town, if I had to choose!'

Now the baby felt some disturbance, and began to wail. She cried louder and louder. I walked away from you, softly swinging her around.

'We'll see,' you said. 'I am going to take you there. You'll change your mind.'

Hänsel und Gretel

— You remember the 'Hansel and Gretel' story?

— 'Hansel and Gretel'?

*— Yes, one of your cruel Germanic tales! The brother and
sister are so seduced by the gingerbread house, they walk
in only to discover a blood-sucking witch waiting for
them!*

It was the baby's first summer and we had yet another new
prime minister. I had been in this country only three years but
had already seen three prime ministers. What would become
of Britain? In the midst of the political turmoil, we escaped.
We flew to north-west Germany, to the Lower Saxony former
mine pit you had found. We had to go to Hamburg first, then
drive towards the North Sea. It was a long trip, but somehow
I was infected by your enthusiasm, and despite my own reser-
vation I felt quite excited too. From the bottom of my heart,
my suppressed romantic sensibility had been woken up by
you, and I fantasised about an enchanted land with acres of
apple trees and cherry blossom. We would have an eccentric
house with a spacious kitchen and great views all to ourselves.
We would grow our own vegetables, and especially my favourite artichoke plants – their large stems and leaves would be so
happy, stretching out freely into the vast country space. I
would probably even hear the sound of their roots growing,
their flowers budding.

We finally arrived at the site. You parked the car, and I stepped onto the sludgy wet soil, carrying the baby. Was this it? This empty expanse of sandy brown soil with a patch of sad grass? My scalp tingled as my hair begun to stand on end. It was very much like the photo – deserted and wild. In the distance, there were elderflowers growing here and there. But they only made the place feel even more deserted. And I could not believe that you had already drawn a plan with such details.

There was an abandoned house on a little hill nearby. The house was dilapidated, the windows broken. An original farmhouse? Or maybe it used to be a lonely farmer's barn which had housed animals before the mining started?

You climbed up on the hill and yelled down:

'Here will be our *Bauernhaus*, with new windows, a new roof and great views looking down into the valley. What do you think?'

'With chimneys and fireplaces?' I asked, and I didn't know why I would ask such an irrelevant question in this situation.

'Of course fireplaces and chimneys!' you cried with excitement. 'We can even build a swimming pool, if you like!'

I stared at you, shaking my head in disbelief.

'It will no longer be the Garden of the Waste Land,' you continued idiotically. 'I will call it the Garden of Earthly Delights!'

Suddenly, the baby laughed in my arms. Her laugh was angelic, though there was also something diabolic in miniature in her impish giggling, which reminded me of her father.

I spontaneously thought of the Grimms' fairy tale – 'Hansel and Gretel'. The brother and sister are abandoned by their stepmother in a forest, and later they find a house built with gingerbread.

'You remember the "Hansel and Gretel" story?' I asked, as you walked back down the hill.

'"Hansel and Gretel"?' You frowned a bit, looking at me as if I were losing my mind.

'Yes, one of your cruel Germanic tales! The brother and sister are so seduced by the gingerbread house, they walk in only to discover a blood-sucking witch waiting for them!'

You stopped, your trousers splattered with mud. Your excitement was quickly replaced by anger.

'But we are not going to have a bloody gingerbread house. And I promise you, I will never force you to bake gingerbread.'

I thought to myself – we Chinese only eat ginger, never bread. It would be your mother baking for you in that witch's house.

Mine & Yours

– When did you start to realise what is yours and what is not yours? Do you remember?

– I don't know. I thought everything was mine until I hit thirty.

The decision was made. Despite my doubt, you were going to buy the German wasteland. You had been talking to your parents on the phone every two days. 'They will help,' you promised. 'But it'll be a while before we can move in, before the house is repaired and the land becomes liveable again.'

I must be patient. I knew that. Of course. But I could not help, in our little rented flat, imagining my daughter running around in her own wild garden, full of newly planted fruit trees. And some Chinese bamboo. Yes, definitely, we would need bamboo. And perhaps a Zen pond too, with floating lotus. Yes, a Zen pond. I imagined what our life would be like, when the day finally arrived.

But still, the child was everything I had for now. She began to walk and babbled a lot, with a hundred mixed-up languages melted into one idiolect of her own. 'Dadadadddaba,' she pointed to her daddy. 'Barhbarhbarbarba,' she pointed to the balloon. 'Yayayayaer,' she pointed to another baby. The more she staggered on her feet, the more she spoke.

When the child was a year old, I took her to a local day care a couple of mornings a week. Since then she had learned more words, particularly words which were often used by her care-givers, such as 'Stop!' 'No!' or 'More!'

One afternoon I bought her an ice cream in the park. She was enjoying it when a little boy passed us, followed by his parents. Noticing the boy watch her eating, she suddenly felt threatened and she gulped down the rest of the ice cream as quickly as she could. Then she shouted, with her mouth full: 'Mine! Mine!'

Mine. This was the first possessive pronoun she had ever produced. Should I worry that she might be self-centred? Or was it natural? To know what is mine means to know what is not mine. But what is not mine, though? I asked myself.

'When did you start to realise what is yours and what is not yours? Do you remember?' On our way home, I asked you.

'I don't know. I thought everything was mine until I hit thirty.'

'So what happened when you became thirty?'

'I learned about failure, and that failure was not the end of everything.'

Failure. Success. Did I see my own life in these terms? In some ways, my life had just begun. Perhaps there would be something there that could be called *mine*, and *ours*.

Rote Beete / Beetroots

– We say two hearts beat as one. That's the reason I grow two beetroots.

– Two hearts beet as one?

Just before you went back to Germany to complete the farm's purchase, I became ill. I was feverish for a few days. Especially when the weather changed and the evenings got dark, I took to my bed, watching the child tottering and climbing around the flat. I didn't feel good. Then you returned from Germany after a short stay. You brought back a signed contract, and a package of goodies from your mother.

'What is this?' I opened the wrapping. 'I hope it's not gingerbread!'

'It's called *Bethmännchen*, a pastry made from marzipan with almond and sugar. Usually my mother cooks it for Christmas, but this time she made it especially for you.'

I said nothing, unwrapping the German marzipan, and taking a bite into the soft mass. It was very sweet, tasted like red bean buns made for toothless people in China.

'Where will she grow up?' I swallowed the soft cake, and could not help voicing my anxiety. 'I mean, she can't be on a farm all the time. Where will she go to school? Which language will she speak?'

'Don't worry. She'll learn German very easily. Children do. And they make friends quickly.'

But I was afraid I would never learn to speak German. Sometimes I thought I should take the baby back to China. I could find a job there. But the thought of returning to China made me feel disempowered and physically ill. I had been uprooted. I wouldn't be able to survive if I tried to transplant myself back again.

You listened to me quietly. You didn't want to indulge in my strange sadness. You said:

'Guess what. You'll love our farmhouse. The moment we signed the contract, my father took the keys and called the builders! I've never seen him acting so quickly and so enthusiastically.'

I looked over the German contract, a thick wad of pages. I felt a little better. I thought perhaps your father was fulfilling his nostalgic wish by helping you to get a Lower Saxony farm, and you were fulfilling your fantasy by projecting our future onto that piece of land. What about me though? Would I fulfil any of my desires through this project? I'd find out.

It took nearly six months before the farmhouse was ready. Finally we moved to our new home in north-western Germany – the Garden of the Waste Land. No, actually, for you it was already the Garden of Earthly Delights. We had a party to celebrate our marriage and our child with your family and their close friends. A few of your German cousins turned up. Of course I didn't have any relatives with me – none of my aunts had a passport. I wore a red dress. A short one with black dots, Western-style. The child also wore a red dress, but a Chinese one. She had learned a few German words from you. *Mutter, das Mutter*, she pointed at me in front of a few guests.

The young apple trees your parents planted were not sprouting yet, but the rock garden you had created was taking shape. Our house was far from finished, but at least we now had windows and a roof. The kitchen was in progress, and we had to cook on a tiny portable stove for the time being. The Zen pond was planned and tons of soil were dug out, but there were problems with the positioning of the sewage and water pipes, which you tried to explain to me a few times. So it remained a hole at the back of our house, gathering rainwater. I often worried that the child would fall in.

Like a farmer's wife, I made a few wooden frames in the garden, and planted beans, tomatoes and artichokes. You were planting potatoes and beetroots – not what I would have chosen to grow in my Chinese garden. For me, potatoes were boring, and beetroots were associated with cold, bleak northern landscapes.

'What's so good about beetroots?' I asked.

'You southerners don't understand them. For me, a good lunch is a red beet soup with a beetroot pudding!'

I was taken aback. So for all this time we had been together, I hadn't made you one single good lunch? All the lunches I cooked for you were wrong for your appetite. Had I been a bad wife from the beginning?

'Well, if these beetroots ever grow, you can make your own beet soup and puddings, I won't. I'm not a *sad* northern German who can only grow things his grandparents have grown before.'

The child on my lap repeated my word: sssaaaaad, sssaaaaad, sssaaaaad.

'Okay, don't take it so seriously.' You looked at her, mimicking her speech. Then you added: 'But don't you know that Venus, the goddess of love, eats beetroots to enhance her beauty. So you'd better eat some of my beets when they're ready!'

I didn't respond.

'Anyway, we say *two hearts beat as one*. That's the reason I grow two beetroots here.'

'Two hearts beet as one?'

This didn't sound like something you would normally say. Perhaps I should study the essence of beetroots properly, and reconsider their importance.

Struggle

*– Why do you want to return to Brexit Britain? Everyone
is struggling there.*
– So at least I can feel my struggle.

It was very quiet on the farm. The patterns of my sleep had
changed. Evenings arrived early. After the child went to bed it
took me a long time to fall asleep. In the morning I woke up
early, earlier than both of you. So early that I could hear the
birds starting their very first dawn chorus. Sometimes at four,
sometimes at five. So quiet, I could hear the woods shivering
in the distance, and the trains beginning their first morning
commute from a station half a mile away from our farm. It was
so still, I could hear your beetroots growing. Quiet, simply
too quiet. Where were the people? I couldn't see myself staying here – with the peace around me becoming like the silence
of a graveyard. I was a Chinese woman, who had grown up in
a hot and populated southern town where activity permeated
every corner of daily life. After only a few months of living in
this valley, like a fish out of water, I was gasping for life.

One morning, we sat by the dining table, and discussed
plans to move back to London. This was not all of a sudden.
It had been lingering in the air from the North Sea, on the
mountain covered by green nettles, down the valley blanketed
by fog, and around the Zen pond, which had never been finished. Once again you asked me the same question:

'Why do you want to return to Brexit Britain? Everyone is struggling there.'

'So at least I can feel my struggle.'

'You don't like the peace and comfort here?'

'I do. But I feel my life has no weight here. I am of no use to anyone, except to you and the child.'

'But I was going to get two ponies and a dachshund for you.'

I fell silent. How could I explain my feelings to you? I thought of the German word you used: *spüren*. It is this *feeling* of life I missed, somehow. On this Lower Saxony farm, even though all sorts of natural life were around me, I did not feel the vigour of life. I wanted other kinds of life. I wanted movement. I wanted the unexpected. I missed the human world, the feeling of struggling and living among other people.

'But you didn't like London before,' you reminded me. 'You said you felt very lonely when you first arrived.'

That was true. But that was my past life. My life as an absolute foreigner in a foreign land. Still, London was the place I had begun my adult life, the place I had finally realised that I had forever lost my parents and my home country.

'Are you sure about your decision?' You studied me, your hands hugging your arms.

'Not totally sure. But one thing is sure – I can't live on this cold farm just now. Maybe when I am older.' Then I added: 'It might take me years to know where we will end up.'

'Or, perhaps never.'

You went for a long walk, alone. I waited. First I didn't wait, I went to check the plants. I thought I should water your beetroots and my beans and artichokes. The hose was long, and entangled like a pile of snakes. It took a while for the water to come through the hose onto the garden. An hour passed, the garden was wet and the shoots were glistering, and I began to prepare lunch. But you hadn't returned. I fed the child and took her to the bed for an afternoon nap. I waited, wondering where you were and why you hadn't told me you would be away for so long. Finally I heard footsteps on the gravel outside. Your boots crushing the pebbles. You appeared in front of the door. When you came in, you took off your muddy boots and said:

'Okay. We'll move back to London, and we'll find a house near the canal.'

At last we had made a decision. We would come back to the farm sometimes, especially when I missed the birds' morning chorus. England would be our Western Chamber, and the German farm would be our Eastern Chamber. At least this way, you said, you would feel better, knowing there was a wild land waiting for us to return to, if the city became too hard to live in one day.

*

Years later, you asked me if I felt I made the right decision. By then, we had already found an old lock-keeper's cottage by the canal in Camden and we had managed to buy the downstairs apartment. I had grown a grapevine by my window, which went up the walls and produced tiny grapes in the summer. I replied, what decision? I thought we had made the decision right in the beginning, even right before we had met. It was on the day shortly after I arrived in Britain, when I walked along the canal and sat on the chopped tree trunk by that mysterious lock-keeper's inn. The decision was made without me or you knowing it. And yet, I still had not met you then. You were there, somewhere not far from the water, looking in my direction, without seeing me and without my seeing you.

Acknowledgements

My heartfelt thanks to: Poppy Hampson, Amy Hundley, Rebecca Carter, Clara Farmer, Fran Owen, Mari Yamazaki, Greg Clowes, Morgan Entrekin, Deb Seager, Justina Batchelor, Claire Paterson, Kirsty Gordon, Juliet Brooke, Cullen Stanley, Carol Gluck, Deborah Levy, Karen Van Dyck, Mark Mazower, Marie d'Origny, Susan Leslie Boynton, Zosha S. Di Castri, Loren Wolfe, Jenny Davidson, Tash Aw, Kaiama L. Glover, Grant Rosenberg, Eve Grinstead, Esther Allen, Patricia White, Fiona Doloughan, Audrey Chapuis, Susan Bernofsky, Kerri Arsenault, John Freeman, Gareth Evans, Peter Florence, Oliver Lubrich, William Wadsworth, Eugenia Lean, Jane Gaines, Peter Connor, Emily Sun, Eileen Gillooly and Lisette Oblitas.

My love to: Anne Rademacher, Lambert Heinlein, Philippe Ciompi, Joan Dupont, Karen Margolis, Thomas Schliesser, Simon Chambers, Simon de Reyer, Jenny Ash, Pang Choi, Vanni Bianconi, Pamela Casey, Therese Henningsen, and, of course, wonderful Stephen and wicked Moon.

My gratitude to: Columbia Institute for Ideas and Imagination; Abigail R. Cohen Fellowship; Columbia University and Baruch College in New York.

Notes on Citations

1. '*Language is a skin: I rub my language against the other . . .*' *A Lover's Discourse: Fragments*, by Roland Barthes, translated by Richard Howard, Vintage 2002.
2. '*How swiftly it dries, the dew on the garlic-leaf . . .*' An ancient burial song from China, author unknown, rearranged in translation by the author.
3. 'Raindrops keep fallin' on my head' by Hal David and Burt Bacharach, for the 1969 film *Butch Cassidy and the Sundance Kid*.
4. '*Ye Yu Ji Bei – Night Rains, Greet the North*', by Tang Dynasty poet, Li Shangyin, liberal translation by the author.
5. '*The awesome but not painful idea that she (mother) had not been everything to me . . .*' *Journal de Deuil*, by Roland Barthes, translated by Richard Howard, Hill & Wang 2012 edition.
6. '*The murmuring mass of an unknown language constitutes a delicious protection . . .*' *Empire of Signs*, by Roland Barthes, translated by Richard Howard, Anchor Books 1983.
7. '*The future's in the air . . .*' Lyrics from 'Wind of Change' by the Scorpions, a German band formed in 1965.